the friendship Matchmaker
GOES UNDERCOVER

Also by Randa Abdel-Fattah

The Friendship Matchmaker

the friendship Matchmaker
GOES
UNDERCOVER

Randa Abdel-Fattah

WALKER BOOKS FOR YOUNG READERS
AN IMPRINT OF BLOOMSBURY
NEW YORK   LONDON   NEW DELHI   SYDNEY

First published in Australia in 2012 by Omnibus Books, an imprint of Scholastic Australia
Published in the United States of America in August 2013
by Walker Books for Young Readers, an imprint of Bloomsbury Publishing, Inc.
www.bloomsbury.com

For information about permission to reproduce selections from this book, write to
Permissions, Walker BFYR, 1385 Broadway, New York, New York 10018
Bloomsbury books may be purchased for business or promotional use. For information on
bulk purchases please contact Macmillan Corporate and Premium Sales Department at
specialmarkets@macmillan.com

Library of Congress Cataloging-in-Publication Data
available upon request
ISBN 978-0-8027-3485-3 (hardcover) • ISBN 978-0-8027-3524-9 (e-book)

Book design by Yelena Safronova
Printed and bound in the U.S.A. by Thomson-Shore Inc., Dexter, Michigan
2 4 6 8 10 9 7 5 3 1

All papers used by Bloomsbury Publishing, Inc., are natural, recyclable products
made from wood grown in well-managed forests. The manufacturing processes
conform to the environmental regulations of the country of origin.

To my English teachers,
Neela Mitra and Nigel Jackson—
you made this possible

the friendship Matchmaker

GOES UNDERCOVER

Stargirl Earth to Potts County Middle School's Friendship Matchmaker! Maybe U missed my last 9 msgs? U usually reply so quickly. Have U got the measles or broken a leg or something? Anyway, that's no excuse. U can't just disappear off the face of the planet like this! Oh . . . maybe U died? Well, even if UR dead then UR family should let people on this site know & not just leave me wondering what I'm supposed 2 do about the fact that Lizzy didn't choose me 2 sleep in the same cabin as her 4 camp. If UR not dead, then ANSWER ME PLEASE!

Paperscissorsrock So obviously I'm desperate, seeing as how U ignored my last msg, and so I'm trying again. Norman had his birthday party at a laser games center & he said he was only allowed to invite his cousins cause it'd be 2 expensive 2 invite school friends 2. So I find out that actually Toby and Juan were invited. So do I say something or is he going to think I'm a stalker?

KidAgainstParent I know somebody who knows somebody who can't stop crying at night 'cause she has no friends to play with at school. What should I do? I mean, not me personally, but what should I tell the somebody who knows somebody to do, to, you know, find a friend?

Paperscissorsrock So have you, like, maybe been struck by lightning or something? So, like, I know there have been storms the past couple of weeks but, like, get undercover will you! Are you there, FMM . . . ?

Stargirl U CAN'T JUST DROP PEOPLE LIKE THIS! THIS IS CAMP. MY ENTIRE FUTURE DEPENDS ON WHICH CABIN I'M IN AND THE ONLY CABINS LEFT ARE

WITH THE DORKS. HELPPPPPPPPPPP MEEEEEEEEEE, FMM!

FMM Automated message: Please note that the Friendship Matchmaker account has been canceled. Apologies for any inconvenience this may cause.

Chapter 1

Right!" Ms. Pria shouted over the noisy class-room. "Get into pairs and start working on the math problems on page three of the handout."

I turned to Tanya Zito, who was sitting at the same table as me, and smiled to myself. The old me would have challenged Ms. Pria on the spot and demanded the right to work alone. But the new me didn't feel the slight-est temptation to take on Ms. Pria. Tanya had already started writing our names at the top of the handout. It was like that now. I called it Friendship Telepathy. When Ms. Pria ordered the class to get into pairs, we didn't need to look around the room for another loner to pair up with. We knew that we had each other.

"Hey, Lara," Tanya said cheerfully. "Don't you just love fractions? I do!"

Tanya is allowed to say nerdy things like this to me now because the new me doesn't bother making up rules and lists such as Acceptable Things to Say at School, or Subjects You Are Not Allowed to Like in Public.

The old me would have whacked her on the head with my pencil case and demanded she keep such dorky enthusiasm to herself.

But I just smiled and said, "I sure do, although multiplication tables are great too."

I sharpened my pencil and scanned the room. I noticed Stephanie nervously shuffling the papers on her desk. She was obviously trying to avoid eye contact with anybody. On the other side of the classroom I noticed Lila Bernard. Her head was half-buried in her schoolbag like a shy tortoise, as she pretended to be sorting through her papers.

I say "pretended" because I am an expert in Total Loner Avoidance Tactics. Total Loners who are forced to find a partner in class are generally too self-conscious to approach somebody and ask to work together. It's a standard protection tactic against being rejected.

So Total Loners will avoid offering to pair up with somebody in the hope that a) another Total Loner with more confidence will ask *them*; or b) the teacher will realize they're in trouble and put them in a pair.

Stephanie and Lila were clearly hoping for either option. But Ms. Pria was too busy writing formulas on the whiteboard to notice their panic.

My insides went all funny. Once upon a term, when I was Potts County Middle School's Official Friendship Matchmaker, I would have sorted out this situation in no time. All I needed to do was find something in common between Stephanie and Lila.

Profile—Lila

1. Not terribly bright.
2. Can be quite sweet.
3. Loves walking and plans to break a world record as the first brunette to walk to China. Trying to

explain to Lila that hair color isn't a world record criterion is like trying to explain quantum physics to a one-year-old. It's just not going to happen.

PROFILE—STEPHANIE

1. Doesn't stop talking.
2. Ambition in life is to be a radio journalist.
3. Finds it hard to make and keep friends because she prefers interviews to conversations.
4. This term she started running Potts County Middle School FM Radio. (Theoretically, our librarian runs it, but who is she kidding? Stephanie has total control.) Actually, I was the one who encouraged Stephanie to channel her lung activity into a radio station. The idea came to me after I'd tried to pair her up with Tanya Zito last term, when I was on a mission to find Tanya a best friend (before realizing I was Tanya's perfect match!). A radio station seemed like a good idea for Stephanie.

A Lila-Stephanie alliance could work. I just had to find what I used to call the Common Factor. In this case, it was easy. They were both obsessed with their goals. At assembly or standing in the cafeteria line, Lila couldn't stand still. She took steps on the spot, clocking them on the pedometer she kept attached to her clothes. She was in training. Since the start of term, she'd clocked 750,000 steps, or was it 75 million?

As for Stephanie, she was happiest when she was talking.

So . . . Lila and Stephanie could walk, while Stephanie talked.

It was so simple it was beautiful.

It was also *so* tempting. But I'd promised myself—and Tanya for that matter—that my Friendship Matchmaking days were over. I mean, I've always had a heart of twenty-four-carat gold, but I had to control myself. If I let myself slip, even *once*, I'd get the matchmaking itch, and before I knew it I'd be back spending my recess running Mediation Sessions and lecturing on my Fashion Rules during lunchtime. And then what would happen with Tanya, my new best friend? I'd have no time for her, she'd dump me, and I'd end up being a loner.

But, boy, was it hard.

So instead of pointing out the obvious to Lila and Stephanie, I turned away and started working on fractions with Tanya.

It was difficult not to scratch my matchmaking itch. But with a heart like mine, I could make the sacrifice.

Chapter 2

Except it felt like I had chicken pox. The more I thought about not scratching, the more my body itched and prickled and twitched. My skin burned as I walked through the playground during recess. It resembled the site of a long and bloody battle. Broken friendships and speared hearts were scattered all around the quadrangle and basketball courts.

Tanya and I were hanging out with Emily, who was dividing up a package of gummy worms we'd bought by pooling our lunch money.

The thing about Emily was that she got along with everybody. When I first started my work as Friendship Matchmaker, I used to categorize people's personalities by color. For example, a person might be fluorescent pink or tangerine orange. You had to be careful who you paired them with because they clashed easily. Other people were neutral shades, or pastels. They didn't stand out or draw attention to themselves, and they could be matched easily. But Emily turned out to be a rarity. In all my matchmaking days, I'd never seen it before.

Her personality was the color white.

She didn't clash with anybody. Put her beside any kid in the lunch line, library, or quad and she easily blended in.

"How many of these do you think you could eat before you felt sick?" Emily asked, handing me my pile of gummy worms.

"I don't know," I said distractedly, surveying the war zone around us. There was no denying it. Potts County Middle School was falling apart.

The teachers on playground duty were rushing around with harassed looks on their faces, yelling out orders to one another as they tried to sort casualties into a makeshift triage system.

"New kid near the monkey bars," Mr. Stirelli

hollered at Ms. Masters as he ran through the playground. "Crying. Suspect ran toward cafeteria!"

"I'm on it!" Ms. Masters cried back, racing to the other end of the playground, her cardigan flapping in the wind.

"Fight in the science lab!" Mr. Stirelli yelled out to Mrs. Ireland, who was busy breaking up another fight between a crowd of fifth-graders.

"What do I do about this crew?" she snapped back.

"Leave them to the student teacher. The other group is critical!"

Mrs. Ireland dashed to the science lab.

"I think I could probably eat about fifty," Tanya said, biting into a blue gummy worm as she examined the remaining half, oblivious to what was going on around us.

"I ate four bags once," Emily said, grinning. "I was sick for hours afterward. But it was worth it." Emily suddenly looked like she'd remembered something. "Can I do the Roald Dahl assignment with you two, by the way?

I was out sick the day everybody chose their group or partner."

Tanya nodded enthusiastically, her mouth full of gummy worms.

Emily turned to me. "Lara?"

Just then I noticed Mr. Stirelli skid to a halt in front of the lockers to the right of where we were sitting. He'd spotted Chris Martin, the school Bully with a capital B, towering over a whimpering Raymond Carlos.

Anything involving Chris Martin needed to be dealt with as an emergency.

Chris Martin had kept me busy during my Friendship Matchmaking days, whether it was comforting his victims or training them in tactical defenses—otherwise known as CMAS (Chris Martin Avoidance Strategies). It seemed to me that since my Friendship Matchmaking days, Chris Martin's pile of victims had grown higher.

The problem was, nobody was safe. Chris Martin was stocky and big enough to take on most kids. That he was great at sports meant he made a point of picking on the non-sporty kids. Not to mention he was a computer whiz, so if he didn't find you during school hours you were cyber-world prey when you got home.

Mr. Stirelli rushed up to Chris and Raymond.

"What's going on here?" he demanded. "Raymond, is Chris giving you a hard time?"

Honestly, what planet did teachers come from? Did Mr. Stirelli really think Raymond was going to tell on Chris?

Sure enough Raymond—Chris glaring at him—spluttered: "I . . . it's nothing, Mr. Stirelli. Chris was just, uh, telling me about his weekend . . ."

Chris smirked triumphantly, and Mr. Stirelli raised an eyebrow suspiciously.

"Is that right, Chris?" Mr. Stirelli asked. "Just having a chat about your weekend, were you?"

Chris grinned. "That's right, Mr. Stirelli."

"Off you go, Raymond," Mr. Stirelli said. Raymond hurried away, a relieved expression on his face. I frowned. Without CMAS, Chris would find Raymond again and pick up where he'd left off.

Tanya tugged at my sleeve. "Earth to Lara!" She snapped her fingers in front of my face. "You're not listening," she said with a pout.

"Sorry," I said with a sheepish smile. "What's up?"

"The Roald Dahl assignment," Emily said. "Do you mind if I join you?"

"Uh, yeah . . . I mean, no!" I shook my head. "Sorry. That's fine."

Emily and Tanya gave me weird looks.

"What's on your mind?" Tanya asked slowly.

"What on earth is Chris Martin doing behind those garbage cans . . . ?"

"Lara!" Tanya cried in exasperation, just as an empty can crashed to the ground. The group of girls sitting nearby screamed, jumping up in fright, and Chris Martin laughed hysterically as he sauntered away.

Chapter 3

The playground was spiraling out of control. Every corner I turned I found kids arguing or teasing each other. The teachers looked weary. And that's saying a lot because as far as I was concerned teachers always looked tired. In fact, one lunchtime I overheard some teachers on lunch duty wondering why they were all suddenly *more tired* than usual. They couldn't figure out why they were going through their vitamins and wheatgrass shots and protein powder drinks so quickly.

As for me, I was struggling to concentrate on my schoolwork and my grades were suffering. When I was Potts County Middle School's Official Friendship Matchmaker, one of the rules in my Friendship Matchmaker Manual had been about brainiacs. I told the smart kids not to be too hardworking or they'd end up getting straight As and be doomed to having reputations as nerds and geeks. My philosophy was that everybody should keep their heads down, try to blend in with average grades, and never "go the extra mile," as Ms. Pria always liked to say we should. Of course, if a kid was really dumb I'd tell them to go as many miles as possible or they'd be picked on for being the slowest kid in class. It was all about playing it safe. Naturally, with my intelligence, I had to hold myself back. But when I threw my Manual away in the girls' bathroom at the aquarium last term, I kissed all my Rules goodbye. Since then, I haven't minded acing my tests or putting in extra effort on my projects.

But with all the suffering around me, I'd kind of lost interest in schoolwork.

"Come on, let's hang out in the quad," I said to Tanya at recess.

The main action was always on the basketball courts, grassed area, play equipment, or quad. I needed to be close to the ground. You didn't become a Friendship Matchmaker without noticing what went on at school. I'd been ignoring the battles around me for too long.

She groaned. "Oh come on, Lara! *Again?* Why can't we go to the library like we always do?"

We usually spent a lot of time in the library because we were both crazy about books and writing. Before Tanya and I became friends, and she'd been a Total Loner, she'd lived in the library. The less visible she was, the less chance she had of being teased. So for her it was self-defense. And she got to read and write and hang out with the librarian. When we became best friends, and I retired from being Official Friendship Matchmaker, I suddenly had recess and lunchtimes free. During my Friendship Matchmaker days I'd been too busy serving the school community to think about myself.

I didn't mind spending time in the library now, though, because we'd go on the computer, read, and swap stories we'd written. But best of all, we'd talk. About everything. Tanya's parents had divorced last term. She didn't say much about it, but when she did feel upset she confided in me.

We liked sitting in the beanbag corner. I'd listen. She'd talk. Sometimes cry a bit. Then she'd feel better and we'd go back to our computer game or books.

But I couldn't keep a close eye on casualties if I was hidden in the school's refugee camp. I needed to be out in the war zone, not where most victims fled for protection.

"Come on," I pleaded, dragging her along.

"Fine," she muttered. "What are we going to do, anyway?"

"Just sit and talk," I said. "Get some fresh air . . ." I'd spotted a sixth-grade girl trying to break into a circle of girls having a conversation, but they were blocking her. What was I supposed to do? Just pretend I couldn't see? Tanya had to understand. She'd been that girl before.

"Can you see that girl over there?"

"Macy?"

"Yeah. She's being left out."

"Oh." Tanya stared at her sympathetically.

"So shouldn't we do something?"

"Like what? We could ask her to sit with us."

"That's not enough," I said, shaking my head. "We have to tell the others off! They shouldn't be allowed to do that to her."

Tanya looked horrified. "It would be brutal! They'd turn on us."

"We need to get them all talking," I said, more to myself than to Tanya. "Sort the problem out."

"You can't force them to like her," she said. "Then it'd be like charity. We should invite her over to hang out with us."

"Huh? Yeah . . . sure . . ." I wasn't paying attention to what she was saying and gripped her shoulder. "I'm thinking a Friendship Intervention Mediation Session followed by an intense conversation boot camp." My eyes were wide as saucers as I thought of all the possibilities.

"No!" Tanya snapped and screwed up her face and stared at the ground. "You can't meddle," she said softly. "People can get hurt, remember?"

She looked me in the eye. I thought for a moment. I understood her completely.

See, Tanya didn't have the backbone to deal with the situation. And why should she? She wasn't popular. I loved her to bits, but Tanya was the color gray. The color of sadness.

It wasn't her fault. Before the divorce, when her parents would fight constantly, she'd come to school with barely a word or a smile. She'd stare out the window. Sniff her school supplies.

Then, when her parents divorced and she had to divide her time between her mom and dad, she withdrew even more. People don't want to be matched to someone unhappy. To someone the color of a bad weather forecast.

I was the only one who eventually saw through all that.

I guess Emily did too, but she didn't count. She got along with everybody.

It was selfish of me to ask Tanya to be brave. There was no need to get her involved. After all, I was her best friend because I cared about her.

˒

The next morning Ms. Pria made us all sit down on the floor because she had a special announcement to make.

"We have a new boy starting tomorrow," she said. None of us so much as blinked. It wasn't exactly juicy news. We had hoped for something along the lines of "summer break will be extended this year" or "free ice cream in the cafeteria."

"His name is Maj—, Majur Mat—, Matak."

That raised a few eyebrows.

"What kind of name is that?" somebody cried out.

"Yeah! Boy or girl? You can't even tell!"

"That's enough," Ms. Pria snapped. "Majur is a boy. A refugee from Sudan. He's come from extraordinarily difficult circumstances, and you will all welcome him with open arms and show him respect and compassion. Is that clear?"

Chris's arm shot up. The glint in his eye told me Ms. Pria was in for it.

"Ms. Pria," Chris said, all wide-eyed and innocent. "Don't you always say you have to earn respect? Shouldn't we wait to see what he's like first?"

Ms. Pria rolled her eyes. "Very funny, Chris."

Chris turned his head to David. "Like maybe see how he takes an upper cut," Chris muttered with a grin.

Luckily Ms. Pria didn't hear. Instead she launched into a lesson about civil war.

Stephanie spoke up. "How can war be civil? Teachers are always telling us to *be civil* so how does that make sense? Hey, Ms. Pria? Did Majur arrive by boat? Where does he live? Has he sold his story to any news outlets yet? Is he willing to be interviewed for Potts County Middle School FM Radio?"

Ms. Pria ignored her (most teachers eventually ended up ignoring Stephanie or they'd be drawn into a debate that never ended) and instead starting yapping away about Majur's life. If Majur was a movie, and Ms. Pria was directing the movie trailer, I figured less than half the class would have wanted to watch him. She was going for the sob story angle when what most kids in my class really wanted was a feel-good comedy, or a bizarre, twisted tale, or a horror movie. What she should have said was that Majur had a tarantula as a pet, lived in a tree, or flew places on the weekend. Instead she went into teacher mode.

She told us that Majur would be an ESL student (and then we got the lecture about how there was nothing wrong with that). Then she told us he'd lost his parents in the war (but wouldn't tell us how or why). Then she told us he was living with his aunt, uncle, and two younger sisters (to which one kid mumbled, "big deal"). And finally she told us that he'd suffered many disruptions and tragedies in his life and that she expected us all to be compassionate and caring and not give him a hard time if he spoke, looked, or acted differently.

In other words, she was *expecting* him to be picked on. I'm pretty sure Ms. Pria was a smart lady, but that was pretty much the dumbest thing she'd ever done.

Ms. Pria was probably hoping to prepare a sympathetic classroom for Majur to walk into. I glanced at Tanya and Emily. They were both listening carefully and slowly nodding their heads. And sure, most of the other kids appeared to be interested . . . kind of.

Then Ms. Pria did the stupidest thing on the face of this planet. She told us Majur was our age but had only been at school up to fifth grade, and even then his school hadn't been like our school. So we had to be patient and couldn't make fun of him for being behind. Some kids broke into giggles, which sent Ms. Pria off the deep end. (Honestly, what did she expect?) A couple of kids got lunchtime detention, and we were all sent back to our desks to do a quiz on water condensation.

Chapter 4

I wonder what Majur's been through," Emily said gravely, as we copied out a vocabulary list in Italian later that day. "I don't know any refugees."

Mrs. Pigorni swept down on us. "Girls," she said sternly, "if you *must* talk during class then speak in Italian. Otherwise, zip it. *Capisco?*"

"Yes," I said.

"Mi scusi?"

"I mean, *si*," I said quickly. Mrs. Pigorni was strict but one of my favorite teachers. She smiled brightly and I beamed.

When she was a safe distance away I leaned close to Emily. "Maybe it's like being in a country where everybody's a Chris Martin," I whispered. (No matter how good I was at school, I could still only talk about the weather, ask for directions, and list food groups in Italian.)

"If he's supposed to be in grade five, how's he going to cope with seventh grade?" Emily whispered back, shaking her head. "That's really crazy. There's no way some of the guys will let him fit in."

She was right. No matter which way you looked at it Majur was doomed to be teased. And I was guessing he'd be so traumatized and messed up he'd sit and take it. He'd be miserable here. What kind of idiots made these decisions? Oh. Yeah. Our school principal, Mr. Muñoz. Not the sharpest tool in the shed (well, that's what I heard my dad say after Open School Night last year).

I was dying to offer my professional help. First Day of School had always been my favorite induction session. A feeling of nostalgia overtook me as I remembered all the kids who'd benefited from a total makeover by me so that they could blend in at school (Emily Wong being the only exception).

Suddenly I felt really emotional. I lowered my head over my exercise book and pretended to concentrate on my work, when really I was jotting down a list.

Why Life Is Better Since I Quit My FMM Days

1. Tanya's my best friend.
2. I have somebody to tell my secrets to and hang out with at recess and lunch.
3. I have someone to talk to on the phone and text.

Who was I kidding? I'd abandoned the needy and desperate all because of my own selfish desire to have friends. Sure, as the school's FMM, I'd been insensitive to Tanya, and both she and Emily had taught me that you didn't have to change yourself to make friends.

But it was a bloodbath out there! Something needed to be done.

The thing is, Tanya and Emily would never understand.

I'd always prided myself on being unselfish, but I had to think about the greater good.

What Tanya and Emily didn't know wouldn't hurt them.

I wasn't going to lie. I'd made a promise that never again would I be Potts County Middle School's Official Friendship Matchmaker.

But I hadn't promised I wouldn't be Potts County Middle School's *Un*Official Friendship Matchmaker.

⌣

It might as well have been Christmas Eve, that's how excited I was when I went to bed that night. I tossed and turned, willing my mom's alarm clock to shriek and for her to barge into my room and shake me awake. Except when her alarm eventually did go off I leaped out of bed and woke *her* up.

I had a plan. The first two people I would *un*officially be helping were Stephanie and Lila. I couldn't stand watching them drowning in their Total Lonerdom anymore. I was going to hook them up and put them out of their misery. And all that was needed on my part was one simple, short letter:

Stephanie, if you want to be an awesome radio journalist you've got to collect great stories! Lila Bernard is your ticket to fame: eleven years old with a Guinness Book of Records goal. What more could you ask for?! She'll be a YouTube hit one day and you'll kick yourself knowing you were so close . . . so why not be the first person in the school—in the world—to follow her through her training? The tears, sweat, and blood. (She was in the nurse's office with an infected blister on her foot the other day.) I bet your ratings will go up from one listener to the entire school and . . . maybe . . . beyond?

I'm just saying . . .

Unofficially *perfect!*

When my bus arrived at school I jumped out and ran toward the seventh-grade lockers. I searched for Stephanie's locker (it wasn't difficult to find—she had homemade Potts County Middle School FM Radio stickers all over the door) and slipped the note into the side hinge.

Then I skipped away to the assembly area. This term suddenly promised to be a million times more exciting.

Chapter 5

Chris Martin was tormenting Louis during science. Poor Louis had been paired up with Chris because Mr. Doyle had zero classroom control. (He was in his first year of teaching and was one of those I-want-to-be-popular types.) Mr. Doyle must have figured that the only way to distract Chris Martin from bullying *him* was to offer Chris some live bait. Enter Louis— proud to call himself a science geek.

Chris had a huge range of tormenting tactics (which is precisely why my CMAS— Chris Martin Avoidance Strategies—seminar was so popular with the seventh-grade population), but today he was trying out something new: meowing and purring at Louis and generally acting like a cat.

In a trembling voice Louis said: "Ah . . . Chris . . . can you please pass me the Bunsen burner?"

Chris, who was standing close to Louis, fogging up Louis's glasses, smiled and then said: "Meowwwwwwwwwww!"

Louis blinked hard. "Uh, please, Chris. We need to keep the temperature consistent."

Chris was unmoved and meowed again. And again. And again. And then hissed and pretended to lick his paws.

The more Chris carried on acting like a feral cat, the more tortured Louis looked. You had to hand it to Chris—he could really go into character. If he used his evil for good, he'd ace drama class.

Hoping to be rescued, Louis's eyes darted across to Mr. Doyle, but he was too busy singing the periodic table as a rap song to notice.

"Tanya, look over there at Louis," I whispered.

She glanced up. "What's Chris up to?" She took a second look. "He's so scary," she said with a shudder. "Glad that's not me paired with him."

"Shouldn't we do something?" I said.

"Shouldn't we do something about what?" Emily interrupted as she joined us with some tripods from the supply closet.

"About Chris tormenting Louis over—"

Suddenly the door swung open and Mr. Muñoz, the principal, walked in followed by a really, *really* tall, skinny boy.

Majur was a giant compared to most of us—even taller than Chris. Majur's black hair was tied up in a ponytail of thin braids. Mr. Muñoz went into the usual welcome-your-new-classmate lecture. Majur stood beside him with an expressionless face and stared at the back wall. Ms. Pria had told us not to expect Majur before lunch, because he'd be in ESL for the morning, but I still couldn't believe our first introduction to Majur would be during a class run by Mr. I'm-so-cool Doyle.

Sure enough, as soon as Mr. Muñoz left, Mr. Doyle clapped his hands together and said, "Hey, man, welcome. In about ten minutes

I'm going to show the class a really awesome experiment. Making an explosion! Oh. I didn't mean . . . you're okay with that? I mean, after all you must have seen . . . you don't need to . . . How about you sit here and read this handout on photosynthesis?"

Oh boy. I felt sorry for Mr. Doyle. He looked mortified.

Majur shrugged and sat down, stretching out his long legs and placing the handout in his lap. He looked down at it and then tossed it aside, more interested in surveying the room.

I noticed Chris approach Majur, dragging Louis by the sleeve behind him. But Stephanie got to Majur first.

"So you've moved here from another country?" Stephanie asked cheerfully. "Africa?"

Chris groaned. "You're such an idiot, Stephanie!" he cried, taking a step toward Majur. "Africa's a *continent*."

Stephanie looked sheepish and was, miraculously, at a loss for words. "I knew that," she mumbled.

Majur blinked and then grinned.

"It's okay," he said, his accent heavy. "I thought you all eating Big Macs all day."

"*Really?*" Stephanie said, taking out her notebook.

"No," he shot back, grinning again.

"So have you ever used a gun before?" Chris asked eagerly. "You know, coming from the war and stuff?"

Majur stared at Chris. "Yes. I like the gun when my cousins annoying me."

"Wow!" Chris cried.

Majur smirked, and Chris realized he'd been outsmarted. He wasn't backing down, though.

"But you must have seen some seriously crazy stuff," he pressed. "Like in the movies. Machetes and guns and stuff?"

Majur looked blankly at Chris. Then he suddenly stood up and walked to the back of the classroom to examine the preserved frogs in the display cabinet.

I glanced at Chris.

There was anger in his eyes.

One thing I prided myself on was my eaves-dropping skills. I had an uncanny ability to hear snatches of teachers' gossip, and it only took me a couple of days of strategically sitting or standing quietly beside teachers to learn quite a bit about Majur. I immediately started to take notes as part of my plan to profile him and find him a friend—something all new kids need help with.

By Wednesday, Majur's profile was coming along nicely and looked something like this:

PROFILE—MAJUR

1. He is from Darfur, which is in Sudan. There'd been a civil war there. I'm not sure what it was all about, but he and his family had to leave Sudan.
2. He lived in a refugee camp in Chad for two years before coming to America.
3. He speaks English but with a heavy accent. Sometimes it is hard to understand him and you have to ask him to repeat himself. On lunch duty Ms. Pria had told Mr.

Stirelli she had to concentrate when Majur spoke to her, and she hoped that she didn't make this obvious in front of the rest of the class.

4. He does ESL (that's help to learn to speak English) a couple of times a week.

5. Majur is Christian. There was a Sudanese refugee kid in grade six who was Muslim. Ms. Pria had wondered if putting them together in an ESL class would be a problem but Ms. Clarity, the school counselor, told her it wouldn't be.

6. He lives in a small apartment with other refugees.

7. His parents are dead.

I started working on a profile match analysis using the complicated data input spreadsheet I'd developed in my spare time over the holidays. As I was calculating Majur's compatability score, Tanya sent me a text message:

I can't sleep. Are you awake?

I was about to reply but then changed my mind. I had so much to do. Plus, there were so many messages on my online FMM account that desperately needed my attention. A pang of guilt went through me as I ignored my phone. I didn't have to speak to Tanya *every* night. I'd see her at school tomorrow.

Chapter 6

I had to drag myself out of bed the next morning. I'd been off-line for so long that the backlog had taken me past midnight to get through. Then, once I'd finally put my head on the pillow, I started thinking about Majur and who his potential friend match could be.

At morning assembly Tanya said, "What happened to you last night? I messaged you. We were going to work out what we're doing on the Roald Dahl project."

"I fell asleep early," I said lamely.

Okay, so midnight wasn't "early," meaning I'd just lied to my best friend. But, hey, there were people out there who needed me. Missing one night on the phone was a small sacrifice to make.

"Okay. Well, I called Emily and we were thinking that we'd do a book trailer for *The Witches.* Emily's mom has a program on her computer. We just need to take photos and collect pictures and write up some slides. Isn't that exciting!"

"You called Emily?" I tried to control my voice.

"Yeah. So what do you think?" She flashed me a cheesy grin. "*We* think it's a great idea. And the best part will be the music. We'll have all the pictures and stuff timed with the songs."

I was upset that she'd called Emily. And I knew I was overreacting, but that's how things happen. First it's a phone call. Next it's speed dial on the cell phone. And then it's a sleepover.

But of course, I knew a thing or two about dignity, so I gave her my most winning smile. "Fantastic," I said, the word managing to push itself past the lump in my throat.

⌒

There was a loud commotion in the seventh-grade locker area. Tanya and I followed the noise to see what was going on. Chris was standing with a group of guys laughing and pointing at Majur, who was picking himself up from the floor.

"What is the problem?" Majur said in a tight voice.

Chris giggled. "It was an accident."

"What happened?" I asked Jemma, who was standing near us in the crowd.

"Chris was walking and smacked himself into Majur. Majur lost his balance and fell."

"Loser," Tanya muttered angrily.

"It was not an accident," Majur told Chris, chin jutting out defiantly.

Chris threw his hands in the air and shrugged, still laughing. "I didn't see you there." Then it looked like an idea occurred to him and his grin broadened. "Don't wear dark clothes! That way people can see you better in the hallway." Chris turned to the other guys. "Ha! Get it?"

The veins in Majur's neck looked like they were going to pop. But he didn't answer. I was about to say something. I couldn't believe Chris could make such a horrible racist comment.

Standing up to Chris when he was bullying somebody had never been a problem for me. I opened my mouth, but Tanya grabbed my arm and pulled me away.

"What did you do that for?" I said angrily.

"I don't think it's going to help if you stick up for Majur," Tanya said to me. "Chris will call him a wimp. It'll make things worse for him."

"Hey, I was just playing around," Chris said insincerely, as Majur started to walk off.

Chris looked at the rest of the guys and threw his hands up in the air, pretending not to understand. "Can't he take a joke?"

I thought Tanya's advice was wrong, but I didn't want to argue with her. So I waited until Majur had left and then glared at Chris and said, "You're an idiot. You're being racist."

He grinned. "I didn't mean it," he said. "I was just messing around."

⁓

Mandy, from our grade, was having a party for her twelfth birthday. She was one of the beautiful people in school, and had her adoring protégés lapping up her attention and doing as she said.

She was popular, pretty, and smart. She knew it too, and so, of course, in my FMM days I'd had to help out lots of girls who'd been caught in her bullying traps. Girls who, in a moment of insanity, had invited Mandy to share a cabin with them in camp and had been laughed at for daring to ask. Girls who had pleaded with Mandy to let them hang out with her at recess only to realize they had to run errands for her (buy her a snack from the cafeteria, return her library books) to earn the privilege of being part of her inner circle. When Mandy cut her hair in a trendy bob, Judy Simons did the same and became the laughingstock of the class. Mandy had silky straight hair. Judy had a mane of untamed curls which, when cut to just under her ears, frizzed out like she'd been electrocuted. When Mandy decided leggings were fashionable, Corine copied her. Except Corine was double Mandy's weight and learned the hard way that figure-hugging leggings were only flattering on certain body types. And Mandy made sure she knew it.

For people like Mandy, birthday parties were

the biggest events on the calendar. Every time I overheard snatches of her conversations with the other girls she was prattling on about what she was going to wear, what her plans were (bowling followed by a makeover party at her house), and what presents she was hoping for. For many girls in seventh grade, being invited to Mandy's birthday was a ticket to popularity. It was a sign you'd made the "in" group.

On Tuesday Mandy approached me after lunch and handed me an invitation. "See you there," she said awkwardly.

It's not that Mandy and I were friends. We didn't even like each other. The truth was that I was invited because as former Friendship Matchmaker I had a certain status with students. Okay, well, maybe that was stretching things. The fact was that being FMM had meant I tended to know some deep, dark secrets. In Mandy's case, I knew a thing or two about her family. She was being raised by her grandparents because her dad was busy traveling the world for business. The truth about Mandy's mom was worse. A court had said she wasn't allowed to look after Mandy and her younger twin brothers. I'd learned all this when I'd had to counsel Mandy's ex–best friend, Thao, who'd since left the school, but not before telling me why she thought Mandy was so nasty. And in the last showdown between Mandy and Thao, Thao had stupidly revealed to Mandy that she'd told me all about Mandy's home situation. The thing is, Mandy told everybody her parents were jet-setting pilots, traveling to exotic locations.

But knowing Mandy's secret had its advantages. Last term I got involved in breaking up some horrible friendship spats between Mandy and another girl, Ramona. As soon as I was in the picture, Mandy became a saint and Ramona was back to being invited to sleepovers.

We'd never spoken about the fact that I knew her secret, but Mandy treated me as extra special and we both knew why. So the birthday invitation was more like hush money in a gangster movie. Which is why I forgot all about it until after school on Friday. Tanya and Emily were at my place, and we'd just finished watching a movie and were sitting on the trampoline, bouncing up and down as we gossiped about school.

"I heard Claudia bragging that she'd been invited to Mandy's party," Tanya said wistfully. "*Obviously* Mandy personally delivered my invitation to my house."

Emily giggled. "Mandy would probably make you come to her house to pick up your invitation."

"It's a bowling party, huh?" Tanya asked.

"Yep," Emily said. "Bowling parties are fun. But I'm not sure about the makeover party."

Tanya heaved a sigh. "Makeover party? Wow . . . that would be like being a pampered movie star for the day."

"Who said we can't be movie stars *now*?" Emily cried, and then jumped up and started impersonating a celebrity smiling for her adoring fans. "Thank you," she said in a snooty voice. "*Of course* you can have my used tissue as a souvenir. It's only *natural* you'd adore me so much. I find it hard enough to hold back when I look at myself in the mirror every day." We doubled over with laughter. Emily bounced back onto the trampoline, laughing along with us.

"Were you invited?" Tanya asked Emily, when we'd caught our breath.

Emily gave her a cross-eyed look that made Tanya giggle. "Yes, but *big deal*. Don't even think twice about it, Tanya. You didn't get an invitation, so I'm not going."

"Really?" Tanya said softly, eyes wide.

Emily shrugged. "Mandy gave me the invitation after school today. But she was so stuck up about it. She just said, 'See you there.' It was like she was waiting for me to scream for joy and kiss her feet." Tanya and I laughed. "It didn't even cross her mind that I might have other plans or might not even want to go," Emily continued. "As far as Mandy's concerned, an invitation to her party means you drop everything."

"I'd drop everything," Tanya said quietly.

That Emily had been invited didn't surprise me. Emily was the kind of person most kids would want at their party: she filled in silences, always had an idea, and could make people laugh with her funny impersonations and accents.

"I'd be the last person Mandy would think of inviting," Tanya said.

"That doesn't mean anything," Emily scolded her.

Tanya flashed Emily a pitiful smile. "Emily, I wish I had your guts. Sometimes what the right people think matters." She shrugged. "That's just the way school works."

"Hey! *We're* the right people!" I said playfully and Tanya smiled. "Who cares what Mandy thinks?"

"That's easy for you to say, Lara," Tanya said. "Just because you weren't invited doesn't mean you're not one of the popular girls. Even though you quit being the school's Friendship Matchmaker, everybody still loves you."

I guess I should have mentioned then that I'd been invited too. But I just couldn't. It would have made Tanya feel even more awful. And I wasn't planning on going anyway, so there was no point in Tanya knowing. Just then Mom called out for us to come inside for dinner and the subject of Mandy's party was dropped. Mom always had good timing.

Later that night I lay awake in bed wondering how to fix the situation. It wasn't fair that Tanya was the only one of the three of us to be left out. What if she found out I'd been invited? If she was invited then the *three* of us could go. Mandy was a stuck-up snob most days, but she had a reputation for the best birthday parties.

So I sent Mandy a text message to say I'd be going to her party. I'd speak to her on Monday and ask her to invite Tanya. Knowing what I did about Mandy, it was basically only a matter of my asking. There was no way Mandy could refuse. It was unfair of me but I figured the end justified the means. And anyway, Tanya was my best friend. I was looking out for her. That was all.

Chapter 7

On Monday morning Majur entered the classroom, surveyed the scene, and chose an empty seat in the back row. Chris pounced.

"Hey!" Chris cried. "That's *my* seat."

Majur looked puzzled.

"But you're sitting down."

Chris smirked. "So? That seat's off-limits."

Majur shrugged and sat down in another empty seat in the back row.

"Hey!" Chris said again. "That seat's mine too."

Chris flashed Majur a triumphant grin and then looked from left to right, playing to the growing audience of kids watching him humiliate the new kid.

But then something strange and surreal and wonderful happened.

Majur slowly walked up to Chris.

Stared at him.

And then punched him in the guts.

After Majur punched Chris, Ms. Pria swept down on Majur and sent him to the office. I faked a stomachache and spent lunchtime in the nurse's office so I could see—well, overhear—what Majur's fate would be. If I was going to help him I needed to keep track of him. Sure enough, Mr. Muñoz's booming voice filled me in and I didn't even need to press my ear to the paper-thin wall. Usually, punching a kid would get you suspended. But Majur was going to spend the next week having his lunch with the school counselor, Ms. Clarity.

This was stupendous news. Majur had sent a kid to the doctor and ended up hanging out with the coolest teacher in the school. Ms. Clarity was the funkiest, spunkiest teacher ever to set foot in Potts County Middle School. She was popular and cool without trying to be.

She was like Mr. Doyle's antidote. You spent five minutes with him and his try-hard kid-lingo vocab and you lost hope for humanity. Then you spent a minute with Ms. Clarity and the world seemed bright again. Chris would go nuts when he found out, especially since the time he was caught hitting someone he was suspended for three days.

Chris missed school for a week. I think it was probably more out of shame than because he was injured. While he was away everybody had a relaxed, dreamy look on their face, the kind of look you get on the last day of school before the summer. Even Ms. Pria seemed less tense.

⌒

"Lara, you can do the section about Roald Dahl's life," Emily said, putting a pencil behind her ear. "About his writing shed and his child-hood. There's loads of research on that."

"Okay," I said.

"Tanya, you can do the summary about the book, plus our favorite parts, quotes, and stuff like that."

"Great!"

"What will you do?" I asked.

"I'll set up the program with my mom and upload the photos and download the images from the Internet."

Tanya clapped her hands with excitement. "This project is going to be so much fun!"

Chapter 8

Stephanie must have read my note because she bounded up to me in the playground and said: "Hey, Lara! I've got an idea that's sure to win me the top journalism prize in the country. Lila has a dream, and there's nothing like having a dream to get people excited."

I beamed at her, delighted with her response.

"Lila's got her heart set on walking to China," Stephanie gushed. "She's agreed to let me follow her around for the next couple of weeks and report from the walking front line."

At that moment Lila joined us, adjusting her pedometer.

"Hi, Lara," she said happily. "Stephanie and I are going to be hanging out for the next couple of weeks. Isn't that cool?"

"Yes," I said, grinning. "Very cool."

I eventually left Stephanie and Lila sitting on a bench (well, Stephanie was sitting and Lila was walking in place). Stephanie had whipped out her portable voice recorder and was already in interview mode, quizzing Lila about blisters and the pros and cons of nylon socks.

I had to hand it to myself—I hadn't lost my touch.

⌣

Although Majur's spoken English was good, he didn't say much, and seemed to be off in another world in class. He sat alone, always at the back, and when he wasn't staring out the window, he was dozing off. It was fascinating watching him fall asleep, his head rolling around side to side and back to front. Once when Ms. Pria was reading a poem, Majur, who'd fallen asleep again, suddenly woke up with a jolt and leaped out of his chair, scaring the living daylights out of Talia, the class actress.

"Oh my goodness!" she squealed, fanning her face dramatically. "You scared me!"

Some of the kids laughed at Majur. Emily

cried out, "Oh Talia, why don't you quit being a drama queen."

Talia giggled and her face flushed red.

Ms. Pria cleared her throat. "Majur," she said gently, "you need to stay awake in my classroom, please."

"Sorry," he mumbled and sat back down, resting his elbow on the desk and his head in his hand.

"As for you, Talia," Ms. Pria said, shooting her a disapproving glance, "Emily's right. Save your acting for drama class."

At other times everybody pretty much left Majur alone. Sometimes there were snickers when a teacher asked him a question or when he asked a teacher something that was obvious to us (like whether we had to copy something from the board).

I was trying really hard—completely under the radar of course—to match him up with somebody, at least during recess and lunchtime. So when Tanya was off at choir practice during recess on Monday, and Emily was hanging out with Bethany, Jemma, and Claire, helping them with their latest animal activism campaign, I hung around the seventh-grade lockers trying to sell the idea of Taking Majur under Your Wing. The plan? Appeal to people's hearts. Get them thinking about helping Majur adjust. David was my first target.

"But he doesn't understand me when I talk to him." David groaned.

I tried to remain calm. "So talk slowly."

"But all I do at recess and lunchtime is play basketball. If I need him to pass me the ball, I can't exactly say that slowly, can I? We could lose the game!"

His stupidity was too much to bear so I left him alone.

My next attempt was Sammy. At first, it looked promising.

"I hung out with him at recess yesterday."

"That's fantastic!" I said. "What did you do?"

He looked at me like I was senile. "We ate our lunch."

"Okay . . . what did you talk about?"

"We didn't talk. We just sat and ate our

lunch." He rolled his eyes. "What language am I speaking?"

"Why didn't you talk?"

"I don't know." He shrugged. "What's there to talk about?"

I didn't bother replying.

After four more equally idiotic exchanges, I gave up. Then I tried approaching Majur myself, waiting until Tanya was safely tucked away in the library so she wouldn't see me in FMM mode.

Majur was sitting on a bench in the covered outdoor learning area, watching a group of the younger kids playing handball.

"Hi, Majur," I said brightly, sitting beside him.

He gave me a funny look. "Hi," he said quietly.

"This morning's art class was a lot of fun, wasn't it?" I said, making sure I didn't speak too quickly.

He shrugged.

Given my experience having conversations with boys lately, I wasn't sure if he was being a typical boy or just holding back because of his English. So I tried again.

"So what's your favorite subject?"

He glanced at me. His eyes seemed to smile for a moment. And then he said, "Home time," stood up, and walked away.

Tanya sent me a text message:

How's the research going?

My response?

Fantastic!

It was easy to lie in a text message. I had to start working on my section of the project soon, but I'd been so busy. If I was going to unofficially help kids, I was going to put my heart and soul into it.

I'd get around to the project tomorrow.

Chapter 9

It's so obvious Majur doesn't fit in," Emily said to Tanya and me at lunch later in the glorious week of our Chris-Martin-free existence. "He just left the class to go to the bathroom yesterday without asking Ms. Pria, and when she realized and he got back, she looked like she was going to lose it, but she must have thought twice. If he's never been to a real school before, how was he supposed to know?"

"Yesterday he didn't go to recess or eat lunch," Tanya said. "Ms. Pria offered to buy him something, but he said he wasn't hungry."

"He just walks around looking lost," Emily said. "But you know what I've noticed? He doesn't have that feel-sorry-for-me look."

"What do you mean?" Tanya asked.

"She means he doesn't act like a victim," I said.

And that's when it dawned on me. I'd been thinking of how to help him fit in from the wrong angle. Majur needed friends, not babysitters.

⌣

The answer hit me in the chest the next day at recess—literally.

Tanya and Emily were in the library working on the Roald Dahl project. I'd made up an excuse—that Mr. Laidlaw needed to see me about my work. They'd bought the story, although Emily wondered aloud why I always seemed to have something going on when it was time to work on the project. I just laughed it off.

I'd been stalking Majur since the bell rang. It had been tricky because I'd had to break up an argument between a trio of girls along the way, help a sixth-grade boy find a group of kids to play with, and remind a girl that wearing her brother's jeans wasn't going to help her join the cool group, which she had her heart set on. Doing all this undercover was hard work, because I had to swear everybody to secrecy and make it look like I was only offering casual advice.

When I eventually made it to Majur, he was sitting on the bleachers near the grassy area, watching a group of sixth- and seventh-grade boys play soccer. I positioned myself close enough to watch him without it being obvious. It was the first time I'd seen him concentrating. They had his complete attention as his eyes followed the ball. I was so absorbed in spying on him that I didn't realize the ball was heading toward me until I felt it thump into my chest.

"Ouch!" As I fell backward, landing smack on my butt, Majur launched at the ball, hooked it on his right ankle, teased it back and forth, and then kicked it back—one smooth, long, perfect kick that (and I swear I'm not making this up) landed straight between the goal posts.

It was the kind of scene that delivers one of those lightbulb moments.

"He can play soccer!" I cried, and then

quickly silenced myself, realizing what a freak I must have looked like.

Anyway, nobody seemed to have heard me. The boys had not missed Majur's moves with the ball and immediately made a beeline to him. Then, in that typical grunt/mumble style boys use to communicate, Majur was invited to join the game.

And just like that my job was done.

⤳

That Majur was a soccer star meant he was in with the sporty kids, and if you're in with the sporty kids in our school, you've pretty much made it. That didn't make him Mr. Popularity in class, though. Off the field, he was still awkward, quiet, and unapproachable. The same kids who played soccer with him during recess and lunch didn't pay much attention to him during class. But when the bell rang, they'd all automatically head to the grassy area and seem to forget they'd snickered at the way he'd read aloud in English, or laughed when he didn't know where Seattle was during geography.

There was nothing I could do about the

situation, so I decided to turn my FMM skills to another cause. I was going to put the unofficial word out that my FMS (Friendship Mediation Sessions) would be starting up again.

There was a lot of work to be done repairing all the friendship problems that had blown up during my time off.

⁓

Chris Martin didn't seem to have learned his lesson because he returned to school looking as menacing as ever. He swaggered through the halls like he owned the place, pushing kids out of the way, "accidentally" stepping on their feet or causing their bags to drop from their shoulders. Maybe he thought acting like even more of a pig than usual would put his reputation back together.

But it was no use.

When he walked into class, Majur, who was sitting in the back row in the seat Chris had first denied him, locked eyes with him, grinned to himself, and then went back to doodling in his notebook. Chris must have thought twice about telling Majur to get out of the chair because he stormed over to another back-row seat.

He'd lost.

And everybody, including Majur and Chris, knew it.

⌒

When the bell rang for recess, Chris jumped up and headed toward Ty and A. J.

"Come on," he ordered. "Soccer time!"

"Yeah, okay," Ty said cheerfully. "I'll get my ball from my locker." Ty turned to Majur. "Come on, hurry up!"

Chris balked. "What? *He's* coming, too?"

Majur stood up tall. "Yes."

Chris looked furious. "You had time to learn how to kick a ball between the bombs and stuff?" He laughed. "Fine, let's see how you play, then."

I had to watch. But Tanya was tugging at my sleeve. "Come on! I've got to buy a snack from the cafeteria today. Let's go."

"Um . . . okay . . . how about we meet at the grassy area?"

Tanya looked shocked. "The grassy area?

You mean where they play *sports*? Since when?" She shuddered. "You know what I'm like around the grass. Isn't it bad enough I get picked last in PE? Now I have to go to the scene of my pain in my free time?" She tugged my sleeve again and tried to pull me along. "Come on, let's sit near the fountain today."

I was stuck. I was dying to see what would happen out there on the field. Suddenly I felt angry. There was so much at stake here. Majur was a refugee! He needed our protection and support, and *he needed me*. Okay, so it was hot, and Tanya and playing sports, or even watching, were not a good mix. But I had a job to do and that meant *sacrifices*. Look up my name in the dictionary and that's what you see.

"Okay, Tanya," I said cheerfully. "You're right. Meeting at the fountain sounds like a great idea. But let's save time. You go to the cafeteria while I go to my locker to get my apple, and then we'll meet at the fountain." And because I knew I'd be ditching her, and I wasn't the inconsiderate type, I grabbed Emily's arm as she was walking out the door.

"Emily, we're going to hang out at the fountain!" I said enthusiastically. "Come with us. I'll meet you both there."

Emily shrugged. "Okay." She turned to Stephanie, who she'd been listening to. "Stephanie, want to come, too?"

Perfect! I thought to myself. *Stephanie will go on and on, and they won't even notice that I'll be gone for most of recess.*

I pretended to head in the direction of my locker but then dashed over to the grassy area. The soccer game had already begun. Majur and Chris were on the field and playing hard.

Chris had the ball and was shifting it to the inside of his ankle, back and forth. Then he flicked the ball to his knee. He bounced it high and kicked it in A. J.'s direction. But Majur was too quick and scooted past, running in and taking the ball. He glided across the field, dodging the others. Chris ran at him, but Majur was like a flash fire. Chris stood panting in the smoke and embers Majur left behind.

"Take the shot!" Ty cried.

Majur and the ball were one. He headed into the corner, kicked the ball. And scored.

His team let out a roar, and some of the kids on the sideline cheered.

One thing was for sure. Majur was born to play soccer.

When the bell rang, the guys high-fived Majur, ignoring Chris. They started walking back to class, patting Majur on the back and cheering him along.

Chris was left alone. He dropped down to tie his shoelaces. The oldest trick in the book.

⌒

"What happened to you?" Tanya demanded to know as we walked into class.

I rolled my eyes and sighed dramatically. "Mr. Smith. Honestly, that man does not shut up. He kept going on and on about this and that, and before I could get away the bell rang."

"Oh, you poor thing," Tanya said sympathetically. "Well, you missed out. We had such a laugh. Emily was doing all these impersonations. She's hilarious!"

"Nice," I said stiffly.

Tanya burst out laughing. "Oh, Lara, you should have been there. I've never laughed so hard in my life."

Chapter 10

For the rest of the week Chris kept to himself and didn't join the others on the soccer field again. Sure he'd push kids around in line, pinch them when the teacher wasn't looking, or copy their work. But he didn't look like he had his heart in it. His usual in-your-face enthusiasm for bullying was missing.

I almost forgot he was around, that's how quiet he'd become.

Until I found a note addressed to me in class first thing the following Monday morning.

Meet me behind the cafeteria when the lunch bell rings.

Chris

The thing is this: it's important to me that my head and body remain one unit. Chris and "behind the cafeteria" was a recipe for physical pain, possible limb ripping and blood shedding. I winced just thinking about the kids who had emerged bloodied and bruised from "behind the cafeteria" after getting on Chris's wrong side, which was pretty much every side of him.

What the heck did Chris want with me?

In the past, I'd been granted a kind of immunity with Chris. I rescued his victims but didn't tell on him, and in return he left me alone. I'm not scared of him and have no problem standing up to him. But, I suddenly realized, that was because I'd always been defending somebody else. I'd never actually been in a situation where I had to defend my own self. I was kind of like a lawyer who has to take the witness stand. I knew I could handle Chris. Experience had taught me that. But I just didn't like how the tables seemed to have turned on me.

Ms. Pria had given us a task for creative

writing, which she did once a week. I think it was so she could pretend to flick through the curriculum or correct our work when she was really writing her own book. Emily saw it one time when she happened to be looking over Ms. Pria's shoulder when she was absorbed in writing a scene in which "Chantelle batted her eyelashes, overcome by Paulo's husky voice."

We had half an hour to write down every thought and memory that entered our minds. I started, jotting down my thoughts and memories as they came to me. They were coming in faster and faster, and my hand couldn't keep up.

- I remember the time I rescued Bethany's schoolbag from Chris Martin just as he was about to pour glue into it.
- I remember the time Chris Martin stole the preserved dead frog from the science lab and stuffed it in Claudia's bag.

- I remember the time Kobe shaved his eyebrows because Chris Martin threatened to shave Kobe's hair off if he didn't.
- I remember rescuing Jack from behind the cafeteria.
- I remember rescuing Suzannah from behind the cafeteria.
- I remember rescuing Josh from behind the cafeteria.

Oh boy.

I looked up from my paper.

Ms. Pria's head was practically buried in her laptop. Most kids were hunched over their desks writing furiously. Tanya and Emily were sitting next to me just as absorbed in their tasks. Emily was even chuckling quietly to herself as she wrote.

I stole a glance behind me. Chris Martin was staring at me.

"Don't forget," he mouthed silently. "Or else . . ." He drew his finger across his throat.

I made a face at him and he looked surprised

(he probably expected me to vomit or faint) and backed off.

So this is what Chris did to kids. Fed on their fear. Put on a macho act. Well, it wasn't going to work on me.

⌒

I was curious about what Chris wanted, but when the bell rang for lunchtime Ms. Pria asked me to help her set up the classroom for art. I walked over to Chris and told him I'd have to talk to him later. He seemed surprised. I doubt he was used to his intimidation tactics not working. Then he made an annoyed face, but by the time he could say anything I'd walked away.

One time I saw Chris's dad yelling at him outside the school grounds. Chris had burst into tears. Another time, at an interschool soccer match, Chris's dad had called Chris a wimp and yelled at him from the stands to run faster.

If you've seen a bully being bullied, it's hard to stay scared of them. I was pretty sure there was more to Chris than he let on at school. So even though I wasn't racing to meet him behind the cafeteria, I wasn't scared or nervous. Not like his other victims must have been.

After dinner that night when I logged on I found Chris had sent me an instant message.

The Terminator Hey! You're not off the hook. Meet me same place and time tomorrow. And come ALONE. PS your profile pic is a shocker.

Chapter 11

When I arrived at school I hovered around the front gates and walked up to Chris as soon as I spotted him getting out of his parents' car.

"Hey!" I said. "Let's get this over and done with. What do you want to talk about?"

Chris looked at me warily.

"Not here," he said, nervously looking around him. "Behind the cafeteria."

"Don't think I'm scared of you," I said. "Maybe this works with other kids, but not me."

He grinned but then quickly wiped the grin off his face, trying his best to look serious and menacing.

"It's okay," I teased. "You can drop the tough-guy act with me. Save it for lunchtime. That's when you work best, isn't it?"

"You talk too much," he said gruffly.

"So what's this all about?" I asked, once we were tucked behind the cafeteria out of sight of the rest of the school population. I leaned against the brick wall and Chris sat down on the retaining wall, in front of me.

"If you tell anyone what I'm going to tell you now you're dead meat," he started.

"Great opening line," I said, grinning at him. "So what's the big secret?"

"I want to hire you to find me a best friend," he said slowly.

I shouldn't have. But I couldn't help it. I burst out laughing.

"That wasn't supposed to be a joke," he said crossly.

"I'm sorry," I spluttered, trying to compose myself. "It's just that out of every kid in the school, you seem the least likely to ask me for help. Since when do you want friends?"

He looked up sharply. "*Need*," he said.

"Huh?"

"I *need* a friend. There's a difference."

"What do you mean *need?* Like a sidekick?"

"You trying to be funny?" he said angrily.

"No!" Suddenly, I felt guilty. Friendship matchmakers—even former ones—had to be there for everybody, not just the nice people. "Sorry. That came out wrong."

He seemed to calm down. "You still doing the friendship matching stuff?"

I shook my head. Outrage flashed in his eyes. "What?" he said hysterically. "You just quit?"

"Something like that," I muttered.

"Well, tough luck. I need your help. I need a friend. And I need one now. Find me one or I'll make your life miserable. Got it?"

"Okay, fine," I said, with a casual shrug. "One best friend coming up."

"Hey! This isn't a joke!" he said defensively. "In case you haven't noticed, Majur has come here and replaced me out there on the soccer field." Chris paced angrily in front of me, throwing his hands in the air. "He's changed everything. Nothing's like it used to be! I was the star player. I get back to school after what he did to me, and there's not a single person who missed—" He cut himself off. "Just find me a friend," he said quietly.

There were so many ways I could have responded. Instead the most unlikely word came out.

"Okay," I said.

Chapter 12

Majur, can I interview you for Potts County Middle School FM Radio? It won't take long. Only recess. And probably lunchtime. Actually, how about you leave the next three days free so we can get up close and personal? I'll do a special broadcast. My Life as a Refugee. Let's start from the beginning. What's your earliest memory? Actually, let's talk about the important stuff first. What is your favorite food in the cafeteria?"

Stephanie had cornered Majur in the locker area at recess. He smiled awkwardly, but the smile quickly turned into a frown and, as Stephanie kept blabbing on and on, he started shuffling his feet, looking desperately around for an exit sign. I saw that as my cue and pushed my way along the crowded corridor, stopping in front of them.

"Hi, Stephanie!" I said. "How's your special broadcast on Lila going?"

She shrugged. "I quit. There wasn't much of a story after all. She walks. And walks. And walks. And that's about it. She doesn't know why she wants to walk to China. She doesn't have a special training regime or diet plan. I couldn't drag a story out of her if my life depended on it. I can't work a miracle!"

My heart sank. My matchmaking efforts rarely failed. Stephanie and Lila would continue being loners in class, and there was nothing I could do about it. I was clearly out of practice.

In the meantime Majur had backed away, escaping Stephanie. I raced after him. Just because I couldn't help Stephanie and Lila didn't mean I couldn't help him.

Okay, so he was a star on the soccer field at recess and lunchtime. But once the bell rang, he became a Total Loner. Yikes! That sounded so mean. My days of Total Loner lists were in the past. But there was no denying it. Majur had all the signs of Total Lonerdom. Everybody pretty much ignored him off the field, and the teachers had to pair him up whenever we had a class project. He was the odd one out. He never did his homework. He was always falling asleep in class. He didn't talk much. He didn't understand any of the work we did.

Take yesterday for example. Ms. Pria had given us a math handout. Majur sat at his desk staring blankly at the sheet of paper. Ms. Pria went over to him and said that he didn't have to do it, and she gave him something else to do. I could see Chris whispering and giggling with some of the guys. Then in English we had to hand in our homework, but Majur said he hadn't done it. Ms. Pria said, "That's okay, Majur, we can talk about it after class."

Chris's hand immediately shot up and he yelled out, "Why does he always get a million chances and we get into trouble?"

Ms. Pria always told Chris off, but the damage was done. Majur's face tensed up, and you could just feel him wishing he could disappear.

Which is why I had to help him out.

"Hey, Majur!" I called out, Stephanie safely out of sight.

He stopped and turned around to face me. "Yes?"

I glanced around, checking that I was out of earshot from the kids in the corridor. "I'm going to offer you some free and unofficial advice," I said quietly.

He raised an eyebrow. I had his full attention. "I noticed you never do your homework. Is it because it's too hard for you? Or maybe in Sudan schools don't have homework?" He frowned slightly but I kept going. "I can hook you up with a kid in the eighth grade," I explained, lowering my voice even further. "He sells completed homework sheets. The best part about it is that you don't have to pay with money. You just have to post something really cool on his online profile on the school intranet, like, 'Jim is the best kid in school,' or something corny like that." I took a step closer toward Majur. "He's got no friends so he's in the business of buying himself popularity."

"And people don't tease him for this?"

I snorted. "He swears people to secrecy and threatens to rat on them for cheating if they tell. I know because once upon a time I was— oh, never mind. Just trust me on this. He's your answer if you're struggling with the homework."

"There is so much homework and rules!"

"All the more reason for me to put you in touch with Jim! He can help you with your homework."

"Thanks," he said, shaking his head. "But no."

I stared at him, confused.

He scratched his head. "It is very difficult. I am not used to it."

"So tell the teachers. They'll understand. Ms. Pria growls and roars a lot but underneath it all she's nice."

He gave me a sad look. "What do I tell her? *Everything* is difficult."

⌣

"Come on," Tanya groaned, as we walked out of class at lunchtime later that day. "Don't tell me you can't hang out with us again? That's the third time this week, Lara. Emily and I have done practically all the work for the Roald Dahl project. We still haven't even seen your part."

I gave her a guilty look. "I know. And I'm really sorry, Tanya. But Mrs. Beggs has been on my case to be Majur's buddy." I sighed heavily. "I'd feel awful saying no to a refugee. He needs my help. I have to get him used to the playground; teach him how to find his way through the library. That could take all year."

Tanya shrugged. "I guess."

"It's kind of strange that they'd give Majur a girl buddy," Emily said thoughtfully.

"Not really," I mumbled.

"Have you at least started your part yet?" Tanya asked.

I couldn't hide the guilty look on my face. "Um . . ."

"Lara!" Tanya scolded. "It's due on Friday!"

"It's okay," Emily said. "How about you organize the songs and we'll do your part? That way the presentation will be in order with the pictures and photos, and we'll just have to add the songs at the end."

I smiled. "That sounds great."

We quickly went through the songs I needed to download.

"I need to go now," I said, sighing with self-pity. "I should get to Majur."

The only reason I could get away with my lie was that the chances of Tanya actually visiting the soccer field during recess or lunch were below zero. She'd have no idea that Majur spent almost every minute of his spare time there, and not touring the school grounds with me as his teacher-appointed chaperone.

Tanya and Emily left to use the computers in the library, where Mrs. Weston was supervising kids doing schoolwork, and I tucked my hair under my hat, put on some sunglasses I'd gotten for free last year, and started searching the playground for Total Loners in need of my help.

By the end of lunch I'd held a mediation session between a warring group of friends and offered some unofficial advice to a new kid in sixth grade about all the ways he could fight back against teasing about his bifocal glasses.

When the bell rang and I'd returned to the locker room, I found Emily and Tanya with arms linked, laughing hysterically. A feeling of jealousy suddenly flooded through me. I'd given up my calling for their sake, and was working undercover, and here they were, acting like . . . best friends.

"What's so funny?" I asked.

"We were messing around with the book trailer and pasted our faces on—" She smiled sheepishly. "Never mind. It doesn't sound as funny when you say it later."

Had we become a trio? And if so, was I becoming the third wheel . . . all over again?

Chapter 13

Claudia, from the classroom next door, slipped a note into my schoolbag as I was walking to assembly in the morning, just as the first bell rang.

"Read it, please," she said desperately. "I need your help—*unofficially*, of course," she quickly added with a wink.

While Emily and Tanya were singing the national anthem during assembly, I sneaked a peek at Claudia's note:

My best friend thinks I'm competing with her in class just because I'm getting better grades than her. Can I see you today? What do I do?

There went my recess.

But deep down I didn't mind. Nobody said this job would be easy.

～

Since the beginning of the year Ms. Pria had been teaching us about how gold was discovered in California. We read about an old gold mining town and how prospectors panned for gold. Then we did an assignment on some famous dead people from the history of that time. So I felt sorry for Majur when Ms. Pria said we'd be playing Celebrity Heads using identity cards of those famous people. Majur hadn't been here long enough to catch up.

It was like that in most subjects. In geography Ms. Pria didn't seem to mind that Majur hadn't done the unit on Antarctica. He did ESL work or she gave him something easier to do. In math it was obvious he was behind with his times tables.

But Ms. Pria didn't mind and never told Majur off. She was patient and understanding and so most of the class accepted that Majur deserved special treatment. The only person who resented this was Chris. And he could still get some of the boys to laugh whenever Majur made a mistake. In English he didn't have a clue about all the fairy tales we'd had read to us since kindergarten. Chris and some of the other boys nearly choked when Majur asked Ms. Pria if Cinderella was male or female.

"Right!" Ms. Pria said. "Tanya, Emily, and David, please take your seats." She turned to the rest of the class. "You can only ask questions with a yes or no answer."

Tanya walked shyly to her seat in the row of three seats Ms. Pria had placed at the front of the classroom. Emily grinned as she jumped out of her chair and confidently walked to hers. David—who always took more time to do something than it took for grass to grow—shuffled from his desk to his chair until Ms. Pria hollered at him to hurry up. All I could think about was why Ms. Pria had chosen Tanya and Emily, not Tanya and me. Did Ms. Pria think they were a pair now? Best friends? Inseparable?

My stomach suddenly felt funny.

Tanya was never the type to put her hand up in class or volunteer to read aloud. She was only really herself around me . . . and Emily. In class she was shy and quiet and hated drawing attention to herself. For crying out loud, she was the color gray! She never stood out.

Seriously, if Ms. Pria ever called on her, Tanya would almost disappear into her chair and her face, like now, would flush bright red. (Some kids had made a point of calling out "cherry face" whenever this happened, which only made her face go redder.)

I tried to catch her eye to offer her a reassuring smile but she wasn't looking at me.

Instead, she was seeking out Emily.

Oh, come on! The supportive friend role? *That was mine!*

Their eyes locked and Emily smiled warmly at her. My heart sank.

"Okay, Tanya, you first," Ms. Pria said excitedly.

"Am I a man?" Tanya asked the class in a timid voice.

"How would we know?" Chris cried out.

"You've always looked like a girl to us!" Some of the kids burst out laughing.

Tanya's face went so red that I wondered if she would burst into flames. She looked at Emily in a panic.

"I . . . I meant . . ." Tanya fumbled and her voice stalled like a manual car sliding down a hill.

I was about to say something but Emily beat me to it.

"Don't be such an idiot, Chris!" Emily snapped.

Generally, calling another kid an idiot, butt face, loser, or other insult aloud in class was guaranteed to get other kids laughing.

Tanya beamed and a wave of jealousy hit me hard.

The game continued, with Tanya, Emily, and David asking more and more questions until all three of them eventually guessed their identities. Almost everybody in class was joining in, calling out answers and making comments. Except for Majur who sat silently, his elbow on his desk, his head resting in his hand. He stared out the window the entire time. Nobody seemed to notice. Except for Chris and me.

I was beginning to think Chris was obsessed with Majur. He seemed to always be watching him, studying him, trying to catch him at something. Listening whenever he spoke in class (which was rare) and eavesdropping whenever somebody spoke to him (which was also rare).

When Tanya, Emily, and David had finished, Tanya sat back down next to me. Emily was sitting at the desk beside us, so Tanya was in the middle.

"That was so scary," Tanya whispered, reaching for her stapler and holding it up to her face.

I took the stapler away from her. "No sniffing school supplies, remember?"

"Oh, yes," she said, embarrassed. We'd broken that habit ages ago, but it had a way of coming back whenever Tanya had a cherry-red moment.

"You were great," I said, patting her on the hand.

Tanya wasn't convinced and gave me a skeptical look. "Yeah, right!" she scoffed.

"Emily was the amazing one!" She turned to Emily. "How did you guess your celebrity so quickly?"

I tried shutting out their voices as they chattered away. I felt I was in quicksand, losing control. This is how you lose a friend. Little things like this add up and pretty soon you've got nothing to talk about or share.

I felt sick. I was about to raise my hand to ask if I could go to the nurse's office—nothing like eavesdropping on the office staff and raiding the supply cabinet to help get your mind off things—but then Ms. Pria called out Charlie's, Chris's, and Bethany's names and asked them to take their turns. She must have thought it'd be easier to stop Chris from heckling if he was in the spotlight.

Even then he couldn't keep his mouth shut. As he walked over to the front of the class, he passed Majur's desk and flashed him a cocky grin.

"What's the point of your being in school if you don't understand a thing we're doing? You should start from scratch. Back to kindergarten."

"Chris Martin, that's enough!" Ms. Pria bellowed.

"Can I go to the bathroom?" Majur asked, ignoring Chris completely.

"Yes, you may, Majur," Ms. Pria said.

Majur stood up quickly and left.

Chris clucked like a chicken and looked from left to right, trying to get the other kids to laugh. But all he got were faint smiles, even from Ty and A. J. who were usually his best audience.

Chris realized nobody was laughing with him and stopped.

It was sad and pathetic. He was sitting at the front of the classroom. The center of attention. Only he was the center of attention for all the wrong reasons.

By the end of the lesson I wondered if I was the only person who'd realized that Majur hadn't returned.

I raised my hand. "Ms. Pria, can I go to the bathroom, please?"

She said yes and I ran out and headed straight to the boys' bathroom. I waited outside until Majur came out. Then I followed him. He sat down on a bench in the quad and started scratching and poking the ground with a long stick from the garden bed behind him.

"Just ignore Chris," I said as I walked up to him. "He's only being mean because he's jealous of you."

Majur looked surprised. "Why aren't you in class?"

I shrugged. "I got bored." I sat down, but not too close to make him uncomfortable. "Hey, what was it like in Sudan? School?"

"Nothing like this," he said, motioning toward the school grounds. "In Sudan there were many more kids in one class and we sometimes had one book to share. It was *completely* different."

"It must be tough here, huh? Trying to catch up? Everybody understands, though. Nobody thinks the way Chris does. He's just trying to get under your skin because you're the new kid."

"I did not go to school in the camps," he explained. "I have missed many years. I know less than half of what you all know."

I smiled gently. "There are people born here

who haven't missed a day of school who probably know less than you!"

He laughed quietly. "You just saying that."

"Seriously. You've got an excuse! They don't.
So don't feel bad one bit." I looked at my watch.
"We better get back or Ms. Pria will have a fit."

"Fit what?"

"She'll be mad. *Really* mad. You don't want
to see that!"

"Sometimes I think if she did get mad and
not give me so many chances maybe Chris
would not be so mean."

I shook my head. "Look, for him it all comes
down to one thing: soccer."

He stuck his chin out. "I'm not going to play
bad just so he treats me better," he said in a
tight voice.

I made a face. "Don't you *dare* play badly!
You do that and he'll *really* give you a hard
time. Right now he looks up to you because
you play amazingly. *That's* probably what
annoys him so much."

Chapter 14

Chris wasn't losing any time. He cornered me in the hallway the next day, demanding to know whether I'd found him a friend.

"Keep your voice down!" I said, worried Tanya, who was within earshot, might hear.

"Have you kept this a secret?" he asked, lowering his tone.

"Yes," I said through clenched teeth. "But for my sake, not yours. I don't want anybody to know I'm doing this kind of thing anymore. It's all supposed to be undercover."

"Good. That suits me fine. So how is it going? Found anybody?"

"It's only been a few days since you asked me," I said, rolling my eyes. "Anyway, I'm still thinking of my strategy."

"Strategy?" His eyes widened in disbelief. "It's not rocket science."

"Would you keep it down?" I muttered in a panic. "Meet me outside at the water fountain."

I walked out, and he waited a moment and then followed.

I leaned over the water fountain and he stood beside me, pretending he was about to also take a drink.

"You need to give me some time," I said. "You haven't exactly been the nicest person in school. Most people don't want to mess with you, so I need to figure out a way to change all that."

"I don't have *time*!" he whined. "The guys are barely passing me the ball in soccer. They don't even invite me to play with them anymore. I have to invite myself. And that's only because I'm not going to let that major jerk—get it? A *Majur* jerk—come in and act like he owns the place."

"Okay, I get it," I said. I took another sip of water and wiped my mouth with the back of my hand. "I'll try my best. Can you at least help me out? Send me a note about your hobbies and stuff. What you like doing."

He gave me a blank stare. "Why?"

I sighed impatiently. "It would help me find somebody to match you with if I knew more about you, wouldn't it? I don't see you getting along with the guys in the chess club."

"No freaks or nerds," he warned.

"Okay, don't get hysterical."

"I mean it," he snapped. "And just because you're doing this for me doesn't mean I won't make your life miserable if you mess up."

"Yes, yes, I get it, you're Mr. Scary."

He tried to look menacing but ended up letting out a laugh. "Look, I only want to be matched with normal people."

There were so many tempting ways to respond. But I bit my tongue.

The more I thought about it, the more I realized I was on an impossible mission.

Chris sent me an instant message after school.

The Terminator You wanted me to send u stuff about myself. This is it.

1. I like sports especially soccer
2. Gaming
3. TV
4. Surfing the net
5. Riding my bike.

That's it. Don't even think of hooking me up with a kid who hates sports and just wants to talk about Harry Potter or vampires. And no wimps either. And forget about any kid who likes sports but becomes a nerd in class. I'm not even gonna begin to think about sitting next to a guy who sucks up to the teacher.

And if you show this to anybody you're seriously dead meat.

It wasn't that Chris's list didn't give me a lot to go on. With any other kid, it would have been more than enough. But I realized when I took out our seventh-grade photos that I had to rule out half the class because I'd be inviting death if I suggested a girl. I started looking through the boys for possible best-friend matches with Chris, crossing them out as they were eliminated. Hakan? He was great with a ball, but he was brilliant at math and not afraid to show it. Somehow I couldn't see him giving up algebra so he could mess around in the back row. Terence? He was obsessed with gaming, which would work, but he had a very gentle personality, which wouldn't. There was no chance Chris would put up with Terence's good manners. Kyle? Chris had pantsed him in swimming last term and didn't let any chance to tease him about it go by. Matthew? Also really into the Internet, but had a weight problem, which Chris reminded us about every chance he could get. Robert? Went pale at the sight of Chris. Charlie? A teacher's favorite, what with his adult vocabulary and interest in world affairs. Tony? Artistic. Marcel? Sci-fi geek. Ali? Into pop music and hated sports.

Eventually I'd gone through every row in the class photo. There were ten boys left who hadn't been eliminated.

It wasn't lost on me, as I wrote down their names, that I was offering a predator his prey on a silver platter.

And while I had a heart of twenty-four-carat gold, I wasn't a saint.

Chapter 15

In all the chaos of Majur's arrival, finding Chris a friend, and taking on my old FMM duties undercover, I'd completely forgotten about Tanya being left off Mandy's birthday party guest list. I only remembered when I woke up on Saturday morning and Mom reminded me that we had to stop at the mall on the way to the party to get Mandy a present. How could I have forgotten to speak to Mandy about inviting Tanya? And I'd already told Mandy I was going!

I acted quickly and dialed Mandy's number.

"Hi, Mandy, I've been meaning to talk to you but I kind of got distracted . . ."

"What's up?"

"Um . . . you forgot to invite Tanya to your

party. Do you want her phone number so you can call her? I'm pretty sure she's free."

"Are you kidding me? My party is today. I can't just invite somebody at the last minute."

"Oh."

Mandy snorted. "Anyway, what makes you think I *forgot* to invite her?"

An uncomfortable pause. I was torn. I cleared my throat. "That's mean, Mandy," I said. And then I thought, what the heck, I need results. "Don't forget I know stuff you wouldn't want other people to know . . ." I instantly felt guilty.

"You're *blackmailing* me to invite her?"

"Hey. This isn't the movies," I said coolly. "I'm just saying."

"Look, even if I wanted to invite her," she said hurriedly, "I can't. You should have mentioned it earlier. My grandma only paid for twenty people. It's all pre-booked and the numbers have already been locked in. Nana will have a fit if I tell her to add another person. Honestly, Lara, there's nothing I can do. I promise I would if I could."

"Okay, well . . . I can't come, then."

"Lara Zany, that is horrible of you! I just told you the numbers are all organized. I've made up games around those numbers."

My stomach plunged. If Tanya didn't go, and Emily didn't go because Tanya wasn't going, and I went . . . bottom line? I'd officially be the world's worst best friend.

There was only one choice.

"Okay, fine, can Tanya take my place, then?"

"*What?*"

"I'm not feeling very good, anyway. Can you call her and invite her? But don't mention that she's going instead of me, or that this is all last-minute."

"Oh, come on!" Mandy wailed. "She's such a dork! Have you seen those revolting clothes she wears? I've got standards with my friends, you know? How can I have Tanya at my party?"

"Hey!" I snapped. "That's not fair! Give Tanya a chance. She's sweet and generous, and for your information, she's actually a great bowler."

"Oh boy," she groaned.

I couldn't help it. I threw out my last scrap of decency and said, "You owe me, Mandy. You know what I'm talking about." I'd backed her into a corner and even though I felt rotten, it was too late now.

"Oh fine, fine, I'll call her now," she said breezily. Her tone didn't fool me. I knew I'd scared her.

I'd probably caused her pain too. But I put that aside and reminded myself that Mandy was a bully. In other words, she had it coming.

⤳

Half an hour later I got a call from Tanya. I answered and held the phone away from my ear, not wanting to be deafened by her excited squealing.

"*Mandy called me!*" she cried. "Oh, my goodness, Lara! Mandy called me and invited me to her party today. Can you believe it? She said she'd been meaning to invite me but had forgotten to give me the invitation."

"Oh, that's great, Tanya!"

"I'm not sure I believe her . . . but it doesn't matter! She's invited me and I'm going."

I congratulated her. It all seemed silly but I had to play along. Then she suddenly cut her excited ranting short.

"Oh, Lara, I'm so sorry . . . I'm so selfish. Look at me bragging about being invited when you weren't."

I choked back a laugh. "Tanya, honestly, even if I wanted to go, which I don't, I can't make it. Mom and Dad are dragging my sister and me to look at kitchens with them today. They're renovating ours." I groaned. "I can't imagine a more boring Saturday. But I have to go. They're really big on all of us having our say."

Sometimes my lies—all told for purely noble reasons—were so good that even I half believed them. "So don't feel bad for a second. Anyway, you know most of the other girls there. Don't be shy and stand back from the group. Get into the conversations. Don't let yourself be left out. Remember all the stuff we practiced? Bunjee Jump Friend? Conversation Openers?"

"Yep, I remember."

"It would have been great if Emily was going but—"

"Oh, but she is!"

"*What?*"

"When Mandy invited me I told her what Emily had done and she said she'd call Emily and let her know I'd been invited and that she could come along now too. I just got off the phone with Emily. She's gone to the mall to get Mandy a present."

It was very tempting for me to roar, like maybe a lion or bear about to sink its teeth into a deer or baby elephant. I'd meddled to protect Tanya, and this is how things turn out? This was my reward? Now *I* was the one to be left out? I quickly got off the phone. (It wasn't Tanya's fault but I couldn't trust myself to not take my anger out on her.) Whatever happened to Mandy's sob story about set numbers and her nana paying?

That manipulative, lying so-and-so.

I sat on my bed, still and quiet, thinking about what I was going to do. Should I call her and demand an invite?

I suddenly felt tired. First the disaster with Stephanie and Lila, now this. Why were all my plans backfiring?

Chapter 16

When you've had a boring weekend, Monday morning can feel like having salt poured into your wounds. Everybody's sharing stories about their weekends—trips to the zoo or circus, baking cookies, or having a picnic in the park—but nothing's worse than listening to other kids talking about a birthday party you didn't go to.

I was in the quad waiting for the bell to ring for assembly. Mandy's party was the only topic of conversation among the seventh-grade girls, who were all crowded around the birthday girl, Tanya included.

Tanya hadn't realized I was close by. She was listening to the other girls squeal and carry on about what presents Mandy got, what the cake looked like, what games were played, what everybody wore, what happened at the make-over party. Tanya wasn't saying much but still, she looked like one of them . . . like she belonged.

I tried to catch Tanya's attention but she was in her own world. I wasn't about to walk up to the group and try to push myself in, so I waited off to the side and pretended to look for something in my bag.

I was relieved when I spotted Emily. She walked toward me and I smiled.

"Check this out!" she said and rolled up her sleeve. She had a huge scrape from her elbow to her wrist. She held it up and proudly examined it. "Dad took us to a new park for a bike ride yesterday. Daniel dared me to go down the hill. So I did."

"Bad fall, huh?"

She hit me playfully. "Hey! Don't you have any faith in me? I made it! Three times, in fact. That's the problem with triplet brothers. You've got to do the same dare *three* times to prove yourself."

"So how did you get hurt?"

"I tripped in the parking lot!" She roared with laughter. "There was tons of blood. My dad freaked, and I was bawling because it hurt so much. And all my brothers could do was laugh their heads off." She grinned. "Of course, it was totally ridiculous when you think about it." She suddenly stood on her tiptoes. "Hey, there's Tanya."

"Yeah. She's with Mandy," I said bitterly.

"Tanya!" Emily hollered. Tanya looked up in our direction and smiled. "Come over here!" Emily bellowed louder.

Tanya skipped over and gave us both big hugs.

"I can't believe you got a strike on your first shot!" Tanya said to Emily. "That was so cool. Did you see the look on Mandy's face?"

Emily rolled her eyes but she was smiling too. "She probably thought I was doing it on purpose to take the attention away from her."

"Probably . . . ," Tanya said with a light laugh. Then she smiled brightly. "It was *such* a fun party. The others let her win in the end," Tanya said, turning to me to explain.

Oh, so now you realize I'm here, I thought to myself as I managed a half smile. I had to play it cool. Even though I was burning on the inside listening to them talk about a party I should have been at too.

"Luckily she wasn't on my team," Emily continued cheerfully. "I wouldn't have played badly just so *she* could win."

Tanya smiled. "I might have," she said. "I wouldn't have the guts to beat her."

"Oh, come on, Tanya," Emily scolded. "I can't see why the others are so in love with her. She can be *so* mean. Donna got her a gift certificate, and she said that meant Donna was too lazy to think up a present herself."

"She was joking, though," Tanya said. "She's very generous. The party bags were amazing. Lip gloss and glitter cream. Did you get nail polish too?"

Hello? I'm here too, you know!

"Yeah. Hot pink. Those bags were the highlight of the party." Emily turned to me.

"Here, Lara," she said, taking out a nail polish bottle from her bag. "You can have mine."

Oh, really, Emily Wong. You can't buy your way out of this. "Thanks," I said, "but you keep it. I'm a nail biter." Then I started biting my pinkie nail, just to emphasize the point.

"Okay," Emily said with a casual shrug.

"She said she'd e-mail us the photos of the makeup shoot," Tanya said happily. "I can't wait."

"The before-and-after photos are going to be so cool," Emily said.

On and on they went. In fact, when I announced I was going to the bathroom, they just nodded and kept right on talking. As if I didn't exist.

⌒

It never worked. There was a pair in every trio. I didn't need my old Friendship Matchmaker Manual with its chapter on trios to remind me that the 33.33 percent ratio was disappearing. And excuse me? Since when had Emily, Tanya, and I become a trio? Emily had been happy to fit herself in with Tanya and me when she was free at recess or lunch. But there were days she hung out with Bethany or Jemma and Claire.

She could be friends with anybody, so why did she suddenly want to steal *my* best friend?

When Ms. Pria said, "Find a partner for your class work," Emily had no problem asking whoever was sitting closest to her. Tanya and I chose each other because we were best friends.

So when did it change? Had we been a trio all along, only I hadn't seen it? Or had Emily simply crept in and stolen my place as Tanya's best friend? Or had she stolen Tanya? There was a difference.

But either way, where did I stand now?

Chapter 17

It was sixth- and seventh-grade assembly on Friday morning. David got a merit award for excellent handwriting. He walked up onto the stage and collected it, a massive grin on his face, and we all clapped and cheered.

Then Ms. Pria started rambling on about how everybody's efforts were recognized but the awards each week were given to people who had tried especially hard. I switched off and looked around me. I noticed Majur sitting cross-legged, his elbow resting on his knee, a bored expression on his face as he stared at the ground. For once he fit in perfectly. Then suddenly Ms. Pria announced Majur's name. I sat up straight, excited for him. But he didn't even move. I don't think he'd heard his name being called. Ms. Pria called his name out again.

"She's calling you," the kids around him said. "Go on. You got an award."

Majur looked nervous and shy and slowly stood up. He dragged his heels toward the stage where Ms. Pria was standing with Mr. Smith, both of them beaming proudly at him. Ms. Pria moved closer to the microphone.

"Majur is being awarded a merit certificate for his excellent reading this week. Everybody clap for him, please."

We all clapped and cheered and some kids whistled but I don't think they were enthusiastic because it was Majur. Any chance to yell and carry on was better than sitting quietly while the teachers lectured us.

Majur half smiled, half frowned. I think he was embarrassed and confused. He took the award and then quickly spun around. He obviously wanted to get out of the spotlight as soon as possible.

After assembly, when we filed back to

class, I went up to him and congratulated him. He laughed.

"What's so funny?"

"It's just a piece of paper. Why celebration?"

I smiled. "It shows you were chosen out of everyone in our class. It's something good."

He grinned then and held up the certificate, examining it closely. "Excellent reading . . . hmm . . . back home if we had certificates it would be for staying alive." He smiled sadly, and leaned closer toward me. "Or for hiding from the soldiers." He lifted the certificate up in the air. "But I take excellent reading. It good." He winked at me. "I like it very much." And he walked away, his head held higher than usual.

I didn't even have time to process what Majur had said because Tanya appeared.

"Can you give us the USB so we can upload the songs over recess? We should be able to finish it before our last lesson."

Oh no. I felt sick to my stomach.

"Lara?" Tanya said slowly. "Don't tell me . . ."

"I'm so sorry! I just . . . forgot."

"But I reminded you on Wednesday night.

And you forgot to bring it in yesterday. And it's due today. You promised! You said you had it under control."

I felt awful. "I'm really, truly sorry."

She took a deep breath. "Yeah, fine," she muttered and walked away.

I had to hand it to Emily. When I told her I'd forgotten, she was totally cool, even though I knew she was angry with me. She just said we'd have to work on it at lunch. The problem was that we weren't allowed to access YouTube at school. We begged the librarian but she wouldn't back down. "Rules are rules, girls," she sang.

Which is why when Ms. Pria called on us to show our project during the last lesson, I shuffled behind Tanya and Emily, knowing that I didn't deserve to stand beside them because I'd done nothing to help. Worse than that was the fact that there was no music. It was just a silent movie of photos, words, and information.

"Put the volume up!" Jackson called out.

"We can't hear anything," Stephanie said, confused.

"There is no sound," Tanya said quietly.

"There's nothing to hear," Emily said, standing tall. "Use your imagination. Uh . . . that's what Roald Dahl was all about. Imagination."

Each second of the ten-minute slide show was torture. Most of the class looked bored and restless, wiggling in their seats or resting their heads on their desk.

Then Ms. Pria covered up a yawn.

That was my lowest point.

When it was over, Bethany clapped enthusiastically, followed by Jemma and Claire. The rest of the class didn't bother.

"That was wonderful, girls," Ms. Pria said sweetly.

I wasn't an idiot. I knew she was doing that "positive reinforcement" thing teachers do so you don't go home and tell your parents you want to quit school and join a circus.

"It really was a great effort. The research was excellent!"

"Thanks, Ms. Pria," Emily and Tanya said.

"Yeah, thanks," I mumbled.

"Maybe some music next time. Then it will be perfect."

I stared down at the floor not daring to meet Tanya's eyes.

"In fact, if you add some music to it I'd love to put it on the school website," Ms. Pria said. "What do you think?"

Tanya and Emily beamed. "Okay, sure!" they said.

"That would be great," I said softly.

"Sorry again," I said to Emily and Tanya after class.

"It's fine," Tanya said bluntly.

"Yeah, it's cool," Emily said.

"I'll do the music over the weekend," I said. "I *promise*."

"No, it's okay," Tanya said. "Emily said it won't take her long to do. It's probably better if we do it because we have the file anyway and we'll know where to add it."

"But then I won't have done anything on it," I said.

"Don't worry about it," Tanya said. "You're so busy anyway. We understand. We'll still put your name in the credits."

Somehow that made it even worse.

Tanya seemed to have forgiven me by the end of the day. She wasn't angry. Well, maybe that's not true. She was probably just too excited about Ms. Pria's offer to put the trailer on the school website to pay me much attention. For the rest of the day Tanya and Emily spent every spare moment talking about the songs and music they were going to use. I wanted to interrupt and make my own suggestions, but I didn't dare. Not after the way I'd messed everything up.

That weekend I moped. Tanya didn't message or call. And it hurt.

I'd been Tanya's best friend. And in that short space of time I'd learned more about her than I ever had about my own sister. I knew Tanya watched *The Sound of Music* at least twice a month. That she couldn't drink out of a can except with a straw. That her favorite snack was barbecue-flavored chips between sliced white bread. That she hadn't given up trying to get her parents back together.

I knew we were drifting apart. But I didn't know how to stop it.

Chapter 18

The next week was nonstop. Suddenly I was overloaded with unofficial Friendship Intervention Mediation Session (FIMS) requests. Mediation Sessions, Bungee Jump Friend, and on and on it went. Kids would e-mail my online account and book me for the next day. Or slip me a note on my way to class and ask to see me. I was swamped. Not to mention that I had to get each person to sign a confidentiality contract. (*I promise not to tell anybody that Lara unofficially helped me.*)

The weird part about it all is that I was dishing out friendship advice when my own best friend was pulling away from me.

Unlike the past few weeks, when I'd had to make up excuses to not hang out with Tanya at recess and lunch, now she didn't seem to mind that I was on "library duty" or was "art room lunchtime monitor."

"Oh. That's too bad," she'd say. But then she'd quickly get over her disappointment when Emily offered to hang out with her. They'd link arms and head out to the playground.

I felt torn between wanting to be with my best friend and wanting to do what I lived for: helping others. I didn't want to lose my best friend. Why couldn't I have it both ways?

So I decided I'd test the waters. See how Tanya would react if I mentioned going back to being Potts County Middle School's Official Friendship Matchmaker.

"Have you noticed how upset Keisha looks?" I said casually as we stood in line at assembly. "She's standing near the water fountain."

"Yeah, she doesn't look too happy," Tanya said. "She's in Mr. Russo's eighth-grade class, right?"

I nodded. "Caitlyn's been spreading rumors about her."

"What kind?" Tanya said, shocked.

"She's been saying Keisha's in love with Joe Marchetta."

"Who's Joe Marchetta?"

"Caitlyn's cousin. He's in ninth grade, over with the older kids."

"*Does* she like him?"

"Nah. Not one bit."

"That's awful. Well, if I hear the rumor I'll make sure to say something. That it's not true, I mean."

"But that's not going to really help her."

She shrugged. "We can't get involved. It'll just make things worse. It's got nothing to do with us. So how come you know all this? I feel like I don't know a thing about anybody."

I drew a deep breath. "Well, you know when I was the Friendship Matchmaker?" She nodded. "People trusted me and talked to me all the time. The other day Keisha told me what was going on."

"Oh, I see," Tanya said. "Poor thing. I feel sorry for her."

"Me too. Which is why I was thinking about helping her out . . ."

She let out a short laugh. "Oh no. Not inter-fering again."

I tried not to look too wounded. "Do you remember those Friendship Mediation Sessions I used to run?"

"How could I forget?" she said, shuddering. "You were so bossy! Telling people what to do and how to act. You know something, Lara? I was dying for you to help me the way you did last term . . . but I was kind of scared of you back then."

My face fell. "Oh."

She gave my arm a quick squeeze. "It's okay. I'm not scared of you now. You've changed. You don't go around telling us all what to do anymore. You just let everybody sort things out on their own. And we can all be ourselves."

There was just one problem with that. Sneaking around like this, watching kids get bullied and not being able to help them out, meant that I *wasn't* being myself.

Chapter 19

One way to deal with a problem is to bury it so deep that you forget it exists.

Well, maybe that's not dealing with it. Maybe that's ignoring it until it digs its way up again. But I just didn't have the energy to get out a shovel. And even if I had, I wouldn't have known where to start.

So I spent the week trying to think about anything but my friendship problems. I threw myself into testing my list of ten possible matches for Chris. It was a total disaster. Nobody wanted to be Chris's friend. I couldn't even sell Chris as a gateway to popularity. Even the loneliest of the lot, Marco, preferred being alone to being close to Chris. I avoided Chris all week, dodging him in the halls, holding

Mediation Sessions in the library where he never ventured voluntarily.

I approached one kid, Samuel, who was sitting alone on a bench eating his lunch, watching the kids in the playground.

"Can we talk?" I said.

He suddenly seemed tense. "What's wrong?"

"Nothing's wrong. I just want to talk."

It was a little sad, the way his face lit up. "Sure," he said with a big smile. "We can talk." Then he laughed, and he was so clearly bursting with relief that for a moment I felt guilty about what I was about to do. Chris had picked on Samuel in the past. Why was I even bothering?

We chatted about nothing and then, eventually, I launched into my Chris campaign, trying my best to sell the idea of Samuel hanging out with Chris. But a shadow seemed to fall over Samuel's face and he sat mute as I blabbered on. Then I realized how dreadful I must sound.

"You're right," I said. "There's probably no reason for you to be friends with Chris."

"Sorry, Lara," Samuel said. "But last term I couldn't get dressed for our weekly swimming lessons without Chris teasing me in front of all the guys for having a girl's body—I don't, by the way," he quickly added. "Okay, so I'm skinny and short but what am I supposed to do about it? I eat like a horse. I just don't put on weight. And, anyway, even if I did he'd hassle me for being fat, like he calls Martin man-boobs."

"Okay," I said gently. "Just forget I asked."

⤙

When I opened my e-mail that night I saw that Chris had sent a group e-mail to about ten kids from seventh grade, me included, with the subject line: Majur is Weird: Comment. That was it. The actual body of the e-mail was empty. Some kids had replied to the group:

Yeah he is a little weird. Off the soccer field. (That was Tony, who always asked Majur to play soccer at lunchtime.)

They say he's seen people killed. He might lose it in class one day! Go after us all. Keep your scissors hidden, hahahahaha. (That was Tim. I couldn't believe it. Tim had only yesterday high-fived Majur out on the field.)

Some people need subtitles, huh? (That was Chris's e-mail in reply.)

You can't tell if they're speaking English cause their accent is so bad! (That was Ali.)

On and on they went. I was furious and sent an e-mail in reply:

YOU GUYS ARE A BUNCH OF JERKS AND USERS. YOU PLAY WITH MAJUR AT LUNCHTIME BECAUSE HE CAN SCORE GOALS AND YOU CAN'T. AND THEN YOU TALK ABOUT HIM LIKE THIS BEHIND HIS BACK. THAT'S SERIOUSLY LOW.

Nobody replied.

My stomach was churning. This was the last straw. What was I doing helping Chris? He deserved to have no friends. I was going to tell him that I couldn't help him. It was too hard to find him a match anyway. I wasn't going to be involved with delivering him another victim on a silver platter.

The first thing Chris said when I told him I was quitting was, "No, you're not."

"Yes, I am," I said defiantly.

He folded his arms across his chest and shook his head. "You don't have the guts to make me angry."

For a second I was lost for words. But then I thought of his group e-mail and got mad all over again.

"You're a bully. You're mean. It's not my fault nobody wants to be your friend."

He kind of lost it then. His face twisted up and he started shouting at me: "That's because they're all crazy about this weirdo! Just because he can kick a ball they forget that nobody plays better than me! How many games have I won for them? And they go and kiss up to this new kid who can't even speak English. They don't even pass me the ball anymore!"

"Why can't two people be good at soccer?"

"Are you *crazy?* I'm the *best* at sports in our grade. And I *am* better than him but they all just ignore me now."

I shrugged. "You can't go around bullying people and then expect them to want to hang out with you."

He grinned. "Tough luck. Anyway, it's all for fun. If he wants to cry about it, that's his problem."

"I'm not helping you. I just want you to leave me alone now."

He stormed off.

Chapter 20

For two days Chris didn't harass me or stalk me online. And it was easy enough to keep track of his movements because things had changed since Majur arrived. Now Chris was almost always by himself, moping around the playground and taking his anger out on other kids, tripping them, calling them names in the lunch line, picking on the smaller kids and making them give him their stuff.

The weird thing is that some kids were asking me to help them deal with Chris. Of course, I had to tell them my FMM days were over but then, when I saw the miserable kids alone, I'd slip them a note of advice (e.g., avoiding a bully is easier than putting yourself in their path and having to defend yourself) or schedule an undercover meeting (first swearing them to secrecy).

I was in the quad with Tanya. Emily was out sick and yes, it's evil to admit but I was glad I had Tanya all to myself. It was like old times, before Emily was in our face twenty-four seven. I was showing Tanya a photo slide show on my smart phone that my older sister's friends had made for her birthday party. We were sitting down watching it, the phone in my hand. Chris appeared out of nowhere, swept down, grabbed my phone and hurled it into a nearby garbage can. Tanya was too scared to say anything. I jumped up and launched myself at the can, reaching down to grab my phone. It had hit the edge and was switched off. It was all scratched and covered in sauce (it had landed in a half-eaten burger). My face went bright red and I turned to Chris.

"How could you?" I screamed. "My mom's going to kill me!"

"Tough," he said, and walked away.

I raced after him. "Are you crazy?"

He turned around to face me. I could have sworn there was guilt in his eyes.

"You forced me to do that," he said defensively, folding his arms. "You pushed me to it."

"Sure, Chris, I wanted you to throw my phone in the garbage."

His body kind of deflated then. "I'm sorry," he whispered. "It's just . . . I need your help."

"But all that stuff you wrote about Majur online."

He sighed. "Yeah, I know. It was mean. I won't do it again. The guys have ignored me since the e-mail anyway. So what was the point? I thought they'd come back to my side."

"Chris, that is just so wrong."

He looked at me guiltily. "I'm so mad, you know? All those guys were my friends. And they just kicked me to the curb when Majur came along."

I didn't say anything, and he searched my face for a response. "Please," he pleaded. "Just give it one more try."

"Fine," I muttered.

The next morning I was standing with Tanya and Emily, listening to them complain about how tired they were because they'd stayed up so late talking on the phone. I felt sick and ran away to the girls' bathroom.

I hid in one of the cubicles and, like an idiot, I lost my cool and started to cry. What made it so bad was that I didn't know why I was so upset. It felt like everything was all messed up. I didn't hate Tanya. Or Emily. I just felt so . . . left out.

I heard a gentle tap on the cubicle door. I quickly wiped my eyes and took a few deep breaths.

"Yes?" I said, my voice wobbly. I coughed and tried putting on a stronger voice. "Someone in here."

"Lara, it's me," said Emily.

"Oh," I said, trying not to sound disappointed.

"What's wrong?"

"Nothing." I dried my eyes and took another deep breath. Then I threw the door open. "What makes you think something's wrong?"

"There's no need to yell," she said.

"I'm *not* yelling."

Even as I was yelling, treating her this way, I knew I was being rotten. But I couldn't stop myself.

She raised an eyebrow. "I noticed you were upset."

Oh. Did you now? Well, Emily Wong, I've been upset for some time now but you've been too busy stealing my best friend to care!

"I'm fine."

"No, you're not. You've been crying."

I put my hands on my hips. "I was not crying. Some dirt got into my eye. I have sensitive pupils."

"Is this about Tanya?"

"Of course not." I sniffed.

She raised both eyebrows this time. "What's going on?"

"Read my lips: *Nothing*."

Emily sighed. "Okay . . . well, if you need to talk . . ."

"I'll know where to go, thanks."

And it's not to you, Emily Wong, I thought as I walked out.

The problem was, I didn't know who to turn to anymore.

〰

Unfortunately, Chris's cyber obsession meant I couldn't forget about him on the weekend. He stalked me online, flooding my inbox with messages demanding to know whether I'd found him a best friend yet. When I eventually logged on to reply, he sent me an instant message:

The Terminator SO? Found anybody yet?

FMM I'm trying my best. It's harder than I thought it would be.

The Terminator I was thinking about it this morning. What about Harry?

FMM I did speak to him. But his eye started twitching when I mentioned your name. That's not a good sign.

The Terminator The wimp. Okay then, what about Turner?

FMM Thought of him too. But you gave him an atomic wedgie while he was wearing his Spider-Man outfit at the book parade last year.

The Terminator Oh yeah. Forgot about that. Stan?

FMM Is it a problem for you that he's part of a creative writing group that meets three lunchtimes a week?

The Terminator Yes. Massoud?

FMM Student council rep.

The Terminator Who's left, then? Don't people realize that being my friend will change their lives?

I hadn't thought about it from that angle. In fact, Chris had hit the nail right on the head. This didn't have to be so painful. I didn't need to make somebody's life miserable just to help out Chris.

If I was smart enough, it could be a win-win situation.

The fact is, I needed to find somebody who was needier than Chris.

Chris needed a friend for a selfish ulterior motive. So I had to find somebody who needed Chris for a selfish ulterior motive too. Somebody who could overcome their fear of

Chris and *use* him as much as *he'd* be used by Chris!

But who?

⌣

The answer came to me the following week, during PE. Mr. Raj had chosen Stan and Rex as captains, and they were about to pick their teams for a game of soccer. Rex had first pick and chose Majur. There was a buzz among the other boys, whispering to one another that they wanted to be on the same team as Majur. I glanced at Chris. His face was tense, his eyes fixed on Stan, daring him *not* to choose him. Stan wasn't an idiot. Plus, after Majur, Chris was without a doubt the best soccer player in our class. Stan quickly called out Chris's name, and Chris went to stand beside Stan, puffing out his chest and glaring at Majur. Majur glared back.

The last person standing was Antony.

Antony was a friendly, happy-go-lucky, simple kind of kid. But he was without a doubt the worst athlete in our class. Even Tanya had more skill with a ball. His claim to fame happened during an interschool basketball match last term. When Antony finally got his hands on the ball, he got a little excited, dribbling it from the halfway line in the court to the basket. He had an open line straight to the hoop. Nobody on the other team tried to stop him. They had no reason to, given he was heading for *their* goal. It was the one time he ever got a ball in the basket.

Too bad he scored for the other team.

So even Antony understood why he was always getting picked last. He wasn't the type to sulk. He just stood, shuffling his feet, accepting his fate.

That's when the beginnings of a plan hit me.

Chapter 21

I logged on to my instant messenger that night. Chris must have been seriously addicted because he was logged on too.

FMM I have an idea. I think I may have found you a possible friend.

The Terminator WHO?

I took a deep breath as I typed Antony's name.

The Terminator R U NUTS? I TELL U I LOVE SPORTS AND U CHOOSE THE WORST ATHLETE IN THE CLASS. I DON'T THINK HE'S EVER CAUGHT A BALL IN HIS LIFE. MAJUR IS TAKING MY PLACE AS THE

BEST KID IN SPORTS AND U WANT ME 2 HANG OUT WITH ANTONY?

FMM Exactly. PS I'd really like it if you stopped shouting at me.

The Terminator I'M NOT SHOUTING AT U. I'M IN MY HOUSE AND UR IN URS.

FMM THE CAPS LOCK KEY IS FREAKING ME OUT. SEE? ISN'T THIS FREAKING YOU OUT?

The Terminator No. But fine. Caps lock is off.

FMM Thank U.

The Terminator Forget Antony.

FMM Hear me out.

The Terminator Fine.

FMM How do I say this nicely . . . ?

The Terminator Forget nice, just get to the point.

FMM You have a reputation for beating people up and acting so crazy that people think UR unstable upstairs and duck for cover when they see U.

I held my breath.

The Terminator U got to the point pretty fast.

FMM Sorry. But we're in a kind of desperate situation now.

The Terminator So what does Antony have 2 do with me being crazy and unstable?

FMM It's not that people hate U. It's just that people are scared of U.

The Terminator Good. That's cool.

FMM Actually no, it's not good or cool when U want a friend. Nobody wants to hang out with somebody who's going to give them a black eye, or set their schoolbag on fire in science.

The Terminator Wimps.

I sighed.

FMM This is what I think: the only person who's going to ignore the fact that U pick on kids is a kid who needs UR help.

The Terminator I don't pick on people. I'm just teasing. Only messing around. Anyway, this isn't about them. It's about me.

FMM WOULD YOU HEAR ME OUT?

The Terminator Now look who's trigger happy with the caps lock.

FMM I know for a fact Antony wants to be good at sports. He hates being picked last. He hates letting the team down. He needs a personal coach. Somebody who can give him one-on-one attention. Kind of like a sports makeover.

The Terminator You just wrote sports and makeover in the same sentence. I just ate.

FMM Do you see what I'm saying? You hang out with Antony, teach him all U know about sports, and UR not a loner any—

The Terminator I'M NOT A LONER! THIS IS NOT ABOUT ME BEING LONELY. THIS IS ABOUT ME FINDING SOMEONE TO HELP ME GET BACK ON THE SOCCER TEAM!

He was shouting at me again. I logged off.

Chapter 22

I eventually persuaded Chris. It's not like he had other options. Antony was his last chance.

The next step was to persuade Antony.

"Chris Martin?" Antony yelled through a mouthful of chips.

"Yeah," I said.

His eyes were practically falling out of their sockets. "Are you nuts?" Then he laughed and wagged his finger in front of my face. "Ah, I get it! This is a joke." He stood up, looking left and right. "Any minute now Stephanie's going to come running toward us to interview me for her dumb radio program. Try to catch me saying something bad about Chris." He leaned toward me. "I'm not that crazy," he whispered.

"Such an imagination," I clucked. "Antony," I said coolly, "this isn't a joke. Just hear me out."

And so he did.

"Let me get this straight," he said, after I'd finished my spiel. "Chris is going to teach me how to play soccer?"

"He's going to teach you how to play all kinds of sports. In his words, 'I'm going to go back to the basics, like catching a ball.' Sound good to you?"

Antony sat deep in thought. As the seconds ticked his eyes widened with excitement. "Actually, it's not a bad idea at all," he said enthusiastically. "It would be awesome to go out onto that field at lunchtime and actually kick a goal!" He grinned. "Where's Chris? Let's get this friendship thing started."

That was more like it. Finally something was going right.

⌒

Tanya, Emily, and I were in the library helping Mrs. Weston set up for the kindergarten book fair. Ms. Pria had asked Tanya and Emily—again assuming they were best friends—so I'd quickly invited myself along.

We were sitting at a desk near a row of bookshelves sorting out piles of bookmarks when Majur came in, slamming the library door behind him. Mrs. Weston was in the back room. The library was pretty much empty.

"If you need a good door to slam," Emily said, "try 5C. It's got better springs and slams beautifully."

Tanya chuckled and Majur gave her a half smile. "I just want a place to sleep," he said. "But the bed in the office is used. And we not allowed in our classroom."

He looked around the library.

"Sit near us and just put your head on the desk," I suggested.

He shrugged like he had no choice and pulled up a chair at the desk near us.

"Did you stay up late?" Tanya asked.

"Yes. I was helping my aunt write a letter for a job. Her English is not so good. Also she is very angry. She has been trying to find a job but they say, 'What is your work experience?'"

He yawned. "We have been living in camps. We don't have *any* work experiences."

"She'll find something," I said gently.

Majur placed his head on his arm and closed his eyes. But Emily wasn't going to give him a chance to sleep.

"What was it like for you in Sudan?" Emily asked. "Ms. Pria told us a bit and I looked some stuff up online about Darfur." She scrunched up her nose. "But there was too much. I didn't know where to start. How bad was it?"

I was embarrassed for her. She had no clue how to be subtle. She must have noticed the disapproving look on my face because she started to backtrack, telling him to ignore her. But Majur raised his head and shrugged again. He was always doing that, like he had so much weighing down on his shoulders and he was trying to throw it off, one conversation at a time.

"It's okay," he said. "Not many people ask. The teachers are too scared, I think. That I will get upset. Except Ms. Clarity."

"Sometimes there are things people think

are too hard to talk about," Tanya said offhandedly. "Not for the person talking, but the person listening."

I felt stunned. Was she talking about me? I'd always listened to her. In this library. In that beanbag corner over there. I felt like I was going crazy. Had I always been a bad friend to her? Or only recently? How would I ever start to fix the damage?

"I live with eleven people in a small house," Majur said, interrupting my thoughts. He sat up straight in his chair. "It is hard for me to do my homework. It is always noisy and crowded. My sisters are smaller than me and they run around. I look after them when I come home. I not complaining. I lived in tents, and worse . . ." Then he grinned. "But there was no Ms. Pria in Chad."

I giggled.

"Do you miss Sudan?" Tanya asked.

"Yes and no. I only know my country in war so I cannot remember much good." He shrugged. "I miss my family. We do not know what happened to some of them. I feel confused here in America. It is a beautiful country. Peace and no killing. Maybe it will take time to feel this is my country too."

"Of course it's your country!" I insisted, Emily and Tanya nodding along with me.

"How did you get out?" Emily asked. "What happened to your family?"

"Is it as bad in Darfur as Ms. Pria told us?" Tanya asked.

He shrugged again. "The rebels attacked my village," he said, his voice slow and quiet. "I saw my friends killed. My family, we running in all directions and escaped. I was with my mother and sisters but we lost my father. We try escape to the border, to Chad. We walked for days. In swamps with big mosquitoes."

I shuddered at the thought.

"We had to hide from the rebels. We were so hungry and there was no water. My older brother, Nwyal, was so thirsty. He did not listen to our mother. He drank the bad water and got infection. He died on the way."

There was no emotion in his voice. But I think I knew why. I think he might have been numb or in shock, like he'd been in a freezer room for so long that he hadn't had a chance to thaw.

"Did you find your dad?" Emily asked.

He shook his head. "No. When we reach the camp in Chad we find out later he was killed."

The three of us were too stunned to speak. Anyway, I wouldn't have known what to say.

It was then that I noticed somebody at the desk behind the bookshelves. I took a closer look.

Chris.

But that didn't make any sense. Chris Martin had to be dragged kicking and screaming to the library. For him to be here voluntarily was serious. Were things really that bad that he'd become a recess and lunchtime refugee too?

He must have heard everything Majur said. The way his chair was tilted in our direction. It was obvious. He didn't even have a book open. Just a car magazine on the desk. We locked eyes.

I tried to read the look on his face. It was a combination of embarrassment, confusion, and guilt. I wasn't going to rat him out. I turned my gaze away, back to Majur.

"Many members of my family were killed. By the rebels. And if not the rebels, by malaria. My cousin died of hunger. Once they dropped bombs on our camp. Many died."

"That's awful," said Tanya, shivering.

It was so awful, I thought to myself, that it didn't feel real. We were sitting in a library surrounded by posters of books about green eggs and ham and a mouse with a cookie, and Majur, just a kid like us, had seen such horrible things. I didn't understand. How did he go from that to lunch orders and school bells? I felt helpless, like anything I said would be dumb. I'm not even sure Majur was expecting us to respond.

I guess Chris must have been thinking the same thing, because when the bell rang a while later and we all stood up to leave he was still sitting, staring at the floor.

That night I was checking my e-mail when I noticed Chris had sent me and a bunch of other seventh-grade kids an e-mail, which was empty except for a link to a website about the war in Darfur. That was it.

*

"Dribble the ball, Antony!" Chris cried. "Control it! Don't kick it!"

"All right," Antony cried back. But he put too much power into his foot and ended up kicking the ball across the grass.

"Try again," Chris said, after Antony had retrieved the ball from under a tree. "You've got to use parts of your foot. Move the ball down the field, don't kick it. Got it?"

"Yep!" Antony's face was bright red but he looked happy.

It was lunchtime and I was at a secluded grassy area in the elementary school section. It was where Chris was secretly coaching Antony.

I was with Emily.

Tanya was at choir practice. Emily had asked me to hang out with her. I told her I planned on watching the younger kids play ball, assuming she'd ditch me for the others. But she'd happily agreed.

I'd positioned us at a bench that had a view of Chris coaching Antony.

It was a funny thing about Chris. Even though he'd call Antony an idiot every now and then, he was surprisingly patient. It was like Antony was his star player and Chris was the coach of the Olympic soccer team.

"What's going on?" Emily asked, motioning toward Chris and Antony.

I pretended I didn't know what she was talking about. But she was too smart for that.

"Come on," she pressed. "What's going on with Chris? He was actually civil all day yesterday. Not one horrible word. Did you mix up some special potion and spike his drink?"

I couldn't help but laugh. I ended up telling her. It felt good to get it off my chest. And I was pretty proud of myself too.

"That's so funny," she said, laughing.

"What's so funny?" I snapped.

"It's a brilliant idea, Lara. Look."

I turned to see Chris and Antony laughing their heads off. I'd never seen Chris so relaxed.

No, that wasn't it. I'd never seen Chris laugh so hard *with* somebody, not *at* them.

I watched Chris for the next week. In class I'd hear him talking to Antony about game plans and rules. "You've got to control the ball. When someone passes it to you, trap it with your leg or chest. Then you can either set up a shot or pass it on."

Ms. Pria kept catching them talking. The first two days of class she was constantly yelling at them. "Chris and Antony!" she'd shout. "Focus on your work."

But Ms. Pria wasn't an idiot. She must have noticed that Chris was so busy talking to Antony about soccer rules and strategies that he didn't have a chance to give anybody a hard time. He was using every spare moment to coach Antony.

In a perfect world, Antony would have been enough. But that's not how things work in the real world. Chris had been hurting. He'd lost his soccer friends and it wasn't something he was going to get over just like that.

When, during PE the next morning, Mr. Raj

gushed about Majur being the best player he'd ever come across, I stole a glance at Chris. His face was full of hurt.

When the bell rang for the end of recess, I walked past Chris and Antony, who'd been playing together again, Chris teaching Antony his moves. Chris waved at Antony to ignore the bell.

"Just take this last shot," he called out.

Antony's face was scrunched up in concentration as he balanced himself, studied his foot and the ball, and then kicked. The ball sailed between their lunchboxes (makeshift goal posts) and Chris jumped up. "Awesome shot!" he cried and high-fived Antony, who grinned proudly.

I followed as they walked in the direction of the classroom. On the way they passed Majur, who was with Chris's old friends.

Majur and the guys were all laughing and shouting, talking about the game they'd just played. Chris's friends didn't even see Chris and Antony, and walked straight past them.

Chris pretended not to notice and put on the

tough-boy act, roaring into the ear of a smaller kid walking in front of them, who yelled in fright. Chris laughed his head off.

He didn't fool me for a second.

⌣

In the IT lab the computer Chris first sat down in front of wasn't working so Ms. Pria told him to sit at the last free one, which happened to be right next to Majur. Chris slowly walked to the chair and sat down, ignoring Majur.

Ms. Pria had set up some exercises on Mathletics. I watched Chris. He logged on and started opening up different menus, instead of doing the work. Then I watched Majur. He looked frustrated. I saw his screen. An error message had popped up. Majur kept clicking on the mouse and keyboard but nothing happened on the screen. The computer beeped every time Majur clicked a button. He gave up and scanned the room for Ms. Pria, but she was busy talking to Mr. Smith, who was standing in the doorway. I was about to get up and offer to help him when I noticed Chris steal a glance at Majur. Then he leaned over, casual as anything, and grabbed the mouse. Majur looked surprised but didn't say anything.

"It's frozen," Chris said, as he pressed some buttons on the keyboard. "You have to press Control, Alt, and Delete at the same time. Then Task Manager opens and you have to do this." He showed Majur what to do, and Majur watched him carefully.

"Thanks," Majur said when Chris had finished.

Chris didn't say anything, just went back to his computer.

⌒

Chris came up to me as we all filed out of the hall when the bell rang for lunch.

"Do you think Antony would come over to my place on the weekend if I asked him?"

"Yes. Why not?"

"I just think it'd be good to coach him for longer than recess or lunch. If he's going to be any good I need more time. Now I know what my dad meant when he used to complain it was torture teaching somebody to play ball when they had two left feet. I think if I had a couple of hours straight I could have him dribbling."

"Just ask him, then."

He paused, a worried look on his face. "What if he says no?"

"Fifty percent chance he'll say yes. So just ask."

⌢

On Sunday morning I was online when Antony sent me an instant message.

Antony I went over 2 chris's house yesterday, can U believe it?

FMM Cool. Did U have fun?

Antony It was awesum. We played soccer the whole tym. Im def getting better thx to chris. His dad came out 2 watch us 2. He laughed @ me everytym i missed the ball. Said i kicked lyk a girl. No offense.

FMM I do kick like a girl. & im pretty good 2.

Antony He played with us 4 a bit 2. Goalkeeper. He said we'd get better when we were challenged. Scared me so i missed every kick. Do U blame me? He kept calling us sissys whenever we missed.

FMM He sounds scary.

Antony U bet.

On Monday morning Ms. Pria asked me to collect the lunch orders and take them to the cafeteria.

"Ms. Pria! I left mine in my locker," Chris called out. "Can I get it?"

Ms. Pria said okay, and Chris went outside.

I walked out the door with the basket of orders. As I rounded the corner of the corridor Chris came up to me.

"Did Antony mention anything to you about him coming over to my place on Saturday?"

"Huh?"

"Did he say he had fun? Did he mention anything?"

"About what?"

"About . . ." He looked up at the ceiling then back down again. "I don't know. Anything . . . maybe about my dad?"

"Nah. Nothing," I lied.

He looked relieved.

"Good," he said and walked back to class.

"What about your lunch order?" I called out to him.

"I don't have one," he called back.

Chapter 23

The school athletics carnival was being held on the sports field in the next town. It was the highlight of the year because it meant an entire day outside of school. We got to play games, have a cookout, and eat ice cream. After the competition we were allowed free time for an hour before going back to school.

When the bus dropped me off at school in the morning I headed to the lockers. I found Majur sitting there alone, staring at a piece of paper in his hand. He looked on edge. His long left leg was stretched out, toe up, while his right leg nervously jiggled up and down. My dad was a leg jiggler. It drove Mom crazy.

"Are you okay?" I asked, as I lifted my bag onto a hook.

"Yeah," he said gruffly. He thought for a moment and then scowled. "Why you always asking?" He started mimicking me (terribly, by the way). "'Are you okay?'" he whined. "'Are you sad? What's wrong?'" He let out an annoyed sigh. "Can't you just leave me alone?"

I stood there and stared at him. "Sorry, but I was just trying to help . . ."

He rolled his eyes. "You trying to help. The teachers trying to help. The government people trying to help." His leg jiggled even faster. "Everybody trying to help . . ."

I didn't move. I just kept standing there, looking at him. I was about to apologize, again, but I was angry. I thought about going off on him, but I felt too guilty. In the end I didn't have to say anything because he broke the silence. "I not going today because I forgot to have my aunt sign the paper." He held it up to show me and then dropped it back in his lap, shrugging his shoulders.

"They will make me sit in the library all today. And you will all be at the sports."

So that was the problem. Who wouldn't

be angry if they had to stay behind while the rest of the class went on an excursion? It had happened to me once. I'd forgotten my permission slip and ended up hanging out in the office while everybody else enjoyed a trip to a farm, shearing a sheep and milking cows.

I took a step toward him.

"Are you *allowed* to go?" I asked cautiously.

He made a face. "Yes. I'm sure my aunt let me. But it's not signed." He shook the paper in his hand. "I hear the teacher yesterday saying that no paper, not going. Not even if your family call to say yes."

I clapped my hands together and went into my let's-find-a-solution mode.

"Why don't you get the office to call your aunt? Maybe she can send her signature?"

He shook his head. "I can't reach her. And no ways for her to send the paper."

"That stinks," I said.

"Huh?"

"That's not fair."

"Yes. I know."

"Teachers and their rules. It's *so* annoying."

"There are rules for everything," he said with an exasperated sigh.

"Raise your hand if you want to go to the bathroom."

"Ask if you want to sharpen pencil."

"Sit down when you eat."

"Never wear a hat inside."

We grinned at each other.

"Back home was not like this," he said.

"Do you miss home?"

He shrugged. "My aunt she says, some people want a home, some people want peace, some people have both in the same place. We had to choose."

"I'm sorry . . . ," I said. I felt tongue-tied by his pain. Not understanding anything about what he'd come from.

He suddenly swung around toward me. His eyes lit up. "Why do people in this country say 'No worry?'"

"Huh?"

He was all animated now. "I say to the man driving the bus, 'I have this ticket, please,' and he say, 'No worry.' I wanted ask him why he worried about a bus ticket." He laughed. "But I didn't."

I laughed back at him. "I have no idea. *Don't worry.* It's just something people say."

"Do you like Ms. Pria?"

"Yeah. Sometimes she can be annoying but she's okay."

"I like her. She treats me like everyone else. Except when I do ESL and see Ms. Clarity. Then I'm different."

I sat down. "Lots of kids do ESL. It's no big deal, really."

"What is a 'big deal'?"

I giggled. "I have no idea! Let's just say you shouldn't worry about it."

"Ah, back to the worrying again."

He looked at his feet. Then he slowly took out a pen and signed the paper, throwing a glance my way, daring me to scold him.

What did it matter? It was a stupid rule anyway. Make a call and give a kid a break. I shrugged. "It costs four dollars," I said. "Do you have the money?"

He fished through his bag and took out some

coins. "Two dollars fifty." He dug deeper. "Fifty-five."

He bit his bottom lip and then looked at me and grinned. "So?"

"So what?"

"*Now* is when you should be helping," he said. "You like helping. So help."

I laughed and opened the pocket of my backpack and gave him the money, part of the money Mom had given me to buy an ice pop.

"I pay you back tomorrow," he said.

"You better," I said.

And we grinned at each other.

Chapter 24

When Ms. Pria asked Tanya to collect all the permission slips and money in homeroom, Majur casually handed his to Tanya. She took it and he stole a glance at me and winked. I smiled.

For the first time in a long time I worried about who I was going to sit next to on the bus. Back in my FMM days, that kind of stuff didn't bother me. I was above all that kind of anxious-nail-biting-who-will-sit-next-to-me business. I was a Loner by Choice, and too busy helping other kids find a bus seat buddy.

But here I was during roll call, moments away from boarding the bus, wondering whether Tanya was going to sit next to me.

I'd figured out that it all came down to that

old saying "out of sight, out of mind." The problem was that for the past few weeks I'd been too busy with unofficial FMM duties to spend much time hanging out with Tanya. Just that morning, after my chat with Majur, I'd been on my way to meet Tanya at the school gates when a kid from the sixth grade cornered me, wanting advice on how to get invited to a birthday party. I could have told him I didn't have time but he was really upset. Especially since the birthday boy had been his best friend last year. So I lost the morning talking to him, and when the bell rang and I rushed to join the line in front of our classroom I found Tanya and Emily deep in conversation. They were talking about who'd been eliminated on *Junior Master Chef* the night before. Since I'd been busy answering messages on my FMM account I'd missed it. So I just stood there.

"Okay, that's the last name," Ms. Pria said, standing up. "Form two lines in front of the door and we'll head over to the parking lot. Stick to the person sitting next to you so we save time boarding the bus."

There was a bit of chaos as everybody paired up. I didn't waste a second. I quickly turned to Tanya and said, "Come on, let's get in line."

Emily was standing beside her, looking as casual and calm as ever as she slowly collected her things off her desk and put them in her bag.

Tanya looked from Emily to me and back again.

"How about we try and find a seat in the back row so we can all sit together?" Tanya said.

"Sure," I said, putting on my cheeriest voice.

"Sounds good to me," Emily said.

Except when we got to the bus Bethany, Jemma and Claire had already hogged the back row and there was only space for one other person.

"I'll sit there," Emily said.

Good idea, I thought to myself, as I sat in the window seat in the two-seater in front of the back row.

"Come on, Tanya," I said, patting the seat beside me.

"Sorry, Emily," Tanya said guiltily.

Emily laughed. "Don't be silly," she said.

Tanya sat down beside me, squashing her bag under the seat in front of us.

I suddenly felt insecure. What were we going to talk about? What interesting topic of conversation could I open with? I racked my brain thinking about all the suggested conversation openers I'd included in my FMM Manual and cursed myself for not making a copy. I'd thrown it out and now all I had was my memory.

Last night's TV shows. (I hadn't watched anything.)

Latest book you're reading. (I'd been too busy to read.)

Gossip. (I couldn't complain about Chris because I didn't want to tell her about my find-him-a-friend project. Really, all I wanted to do was to complain about Emily, but that wasn't exactly an option.)

Interesting facts and trivia.

Luckily for me my sister was doing a school science project and had been practicing her speech with the family at dinnertime.

173

"Hey, Tanya," I said, "do you know that the most dangerous animal in the world is the house fly? 'Cause they love poop, they spread more diseases than any other animal."

"Really?" Tanya said in a distracted tone.

Okay, not the most exciting conversation opener but for once I was stuck.

"Yep," I said lamely.

"Dad's getting me a puppy," Tanya said.

"Cool," I said.

"He said I can choose whatever puppy I like. We're going to the pet shop tomorrow." She folded her knees on the seat and turned around to face Emily behind us.

"So what kind of puppy do you think I should get? I can't remember the name you told me."

I didn't want to be left out so I got onto my knees and turned around too.

"Labradors are adorable. Maltese are cute too. It's so hard to choose, though."

"My dad wouldn't have a clue," Tanya said. "And I don't know anything about dogs."

"Me either," I said. Dumb move.

"Okay," Emily said. "If you want I can come with you to the pet shop tomorrow."

Tanya grinned. "That would be awesome!"

"I can't stay long because it's my gran's birthday, but I'm sure Mom won't mind taking me. I'll meet you at the store, and then we can go to my gran's from there."

I waited for Tanya to invite me too.

But she didn't.

Bethany, Jemma, and Claire, all madly-in-love-with-animals types, heard "new puppy" and went crazy. For the rest of the bus trip the five of them talked about puppies.

I had nothing to say.

"Um . . . I feel carsick facing backward," I eventually mumbled and slumped down into my seat.

"Here, have some water," Tanya said gently, handing me her bottle.

I took it from her but she'd turned away again, facing backward talking with the others.

I lifted myself up off the seat and surveyed the bus. Majur was sitting beside Ty. I could make out that they were talking about some sport. Antony was sitting next to Chris reading a book called *The Rules of Soccer*, which I'd overheard Chris order him to memorize.

Everybody was pretty much chatting happily to somebody else.

There were only two people who had nobody to talk to.

Chris.

And me.

⌒

When we arrived we dumped our bags and waited for the teachers to split us into teams. I stood next to Tanya, praying that the teachers would put us together. Ms. Pria and Mrs. Weston stood up front for roll call and then started assigning everybody to house teams. Chris and Antony were put in the same house, Tigers. Majur was put in Grizzlies. I was put in Cougars. When Ms. Pria called out Emily's name I squeezed my eyes shut for a second.

"Bobcats," she said.

Then Ms. Pria called out Tanya's name.

Not Bobcats. Not Bobcats. Not Bobcats.

"Bobcats," she said.

Panic swamped me.

"That's not fair," Tanya said, pouting. "They've separated the three of us."

"Yeah," I mumbled. "See you at lunch."

At least she remembered me enough to give me a sympathetic look before joining Emily.

The first part of the day was spent on the track events. Emily loved sports, and I wasn't bad either, and we both collected a couple of blue ribbons. But I could see Tanya struggling, coming in last in almost every event. She had a tortured look on her face.

When it was finally lunchtime and the competition was over, I met up with Tanya and Emily. The teachers had cooked hot dogs and we were lined up to collect our buns when Ms. Pria announced that our class would play a game of soccer after lunch.

"No houses," she said. "It will just be our class."

"Do we have to play?" Tanya pleaded, when we approached the table.

"Yes," Ms. Pria said. "*Everybody* is joining in." She slapped her hands together and flashed Tanya a big smile. "Today is about fun and fitness, Tanya. You *will* have fun and you *will* get fit!"

"Yeah, sure," Tanya muttered to me. "More like I'll drop the ball and people will *make fun of me*."

Emily beat me to it and patted Tanya on the arm. "You'll be fine," she said.

∽

Samuel won the toss and took the kickoff. He ran down the field, teasing the ball, tossing it from his right ankle to his left. Tanya, who was on Samuel's team, shrieked as he headed in her direction. She jumped out of his way, a look of relief on her face.

Samuel passed the ball to Lila (whose walking obsession made her one of the fittest in our class), and she traveled halfway down the field with it, passing it to Emily who hovered near the side.

Emily, the ball landing at her feet, took possession. David charged toward the ball and Emily kicked it hard along the ground all the way to Terry. But Pamela was too slow and

Majur slid in front of her and kicked the ball to Omar. The ball flew through the air a few inches off the ground. Omar caught the ball with the side of his foot, lined it up for a goal, and kicked with all his might. The ball sailed past Jemma and landed in the goal. Majur's team grinned and cheered and pumped their fists into the air, teasing Chris's team.

It was all good fun and standard behavior (I'd seen Chris do more to rub it in) but that it was *Majur's* team that was winning and Majur who was running around letting out happy hoots with the rest of his team made it a million times worse for Chris.

On the soccer field Majur wasn't a refugee. There was no room for feeling sorry for him. He was just another soccer player.

We called time and Chris gathered us around him in a huddle.

"This is crazy! They're winning. We're better than that! Antony, you've gotta go for the ball. Chase it! I told you your best talent is your speed. Just get possession, kick it to me, and leave the fancy ballwork to me and

179

the others. But you gotta get onto Majur. He's too fast for the rest of us!"

On and on he went. I had to hand it to him, he knew the game inside out. He knew what it meant to work as a team. Out on the field he was a different person from the obnoxious pig he could be in the halls and classroom.

Ms. Pria blew the whistle and the game began again. Lila stopped and stepped back on her left foot ready for a big kick. She looked in Majur's direction and kicked the ball straight to him.

"Chase him!" Chris yelled out to Antony.

Majur trapped the ball with his leg and then kicked the ball to Ty before Antony could intercept. But he kicked too high and Chris cut into Ty's advance, stealing the ball in one smooth move and dribbling it past A. J. and Jackson.

Then, miraculously, Antony latched onto a perfect long pass from Chris. Ty yelled out, "Stop him!" to Bart, who was playing keeper. But Antony played the ball past Bart, and lined up his kick. Chris went crazy.

"You've got it!" he screamed, punching the air with his fist. "You've got it!"

And he would have had it. Only Antony got a bit too excited and ran up to the ball. He was going to try and blast it in.

"No!" Chris yelled.

But it was too late. Antony kicked with all his might and the ball, which was an easy gentle kick into the goal, sailed up high and missed.

The class went crazy.

Ty, A. J., David, Bart, and Terry all burst into hysterical laughter, leaning on one another for support as their bodies shook. Even Majur was laughing.

They hooted and shrieked with laughter, pointing at Antony.

Antony was shattered.

"Chris, man!" Ty cried out, laughing as he stumbled over toward Chris and put his arm around his shoulders. "That was tragic!" he spluttered sympathetically. "You lined it up for him and he killed it!" The others burst into another round of laughter. Antony was standing alone, silent, a look of shame on his

181

face. A. J. and the others stood around Chris, offering words of support, as they joked and made fun of Antony.

Everything had suddenly changed. Antony's mess-up had brought Chris back into the group.

I studied Chris's face. For a second his eyes flickered with relief. I realized it had been a long time since I'd seen the guys rally around him like that. Talk to him. Notice him. No wonder Chris started to grin.

I looked over at Antony. His face fell as he stared at Chris. Then he turned away, dragging his feet over the grass toward the sideline.

My heart broke for him.

The guys were still laughing and joking around. I stared at them again. And that's when I noticed Chris's face change. He looked over at Antony, sitting on the bench, head down. He looked at Ty, A. J., and the others.

And he walked away.

To sit beside Antony.

Chris let his hand fall on Antony's shoulder for one moment. And then he apologized.

Like a true friend would.

Chapter 25

Stephanie sat beside me in the back room of the library, the recorder on the desk between us.

"Okay, so what's this all about?" she asked.

"I just need a couple of minutes of the program to send out a message."

"So what should my intro be?"

I ran my fingers through my hair. "Um, this is a message from Potts County Middle School's Former Official Friendship Matchmaker."

Stephanie's face brightened. "Ooh! Sounds dramatic." She cleared her throat and took a massive gulp from her water bottle. "Okay, ready?"

I nodded and she pressed the record button, grinned at me, and started: "Hello to Potts County Middle School. Today we have a *very*

special guest. The one and only Lara Zany. Anybody who's anybody would know that last year Lara quit her role as this school's Official Friendship Matchmaker. Naturally we were all devastated. Almost everybody knows somebody who's been helped by Lara. Believe it or not even I've been lucky enough to have had Lara help me . . ."

I tried not to groan and sat patiently waiting for silence. I'd decided to set the record straight and send out one last message to everybody at school, hoping Tanya would understand.

". . . and she taught me and others . . ."

And, just maybe, forgive me. Yet again.

"Over to Lara!"

I looked up, startled. "Oh, okay," I stumbled, smoothing out the piece of paper I'd written my speech on.

"It's all yours!" Stephanie said cheerfully, edging the recorder closer to me.

"Um, well, hi, everybody," I said. I cleared my throat, took a deep breath, and started to read. "Some of you know I've been helping out at the playground again . . . kind of doing some unofficial friendship matchmaking . . . I know there are some people, well, one person, who'd be hurt to know this, especially that I didn't tell her. If you're listening I just want to say I'm sorry. I didn't mean to go behind your back. I was just trying to help people, but I know I put everybody else before our friendship and ignored you a lot. So, um, sorry.

"I also want to let everybody know I've closed my FMM account for the second and last time. But this time you all deserve to know why. It's not because I don't care. It's because I don't have the answers. I kind of only thought I did. And believe it or not, it took a bully to show me that.

"I do know two things, though. The first is that nobody is always good. Or always bad." I let out a short laugh. "Except in the movies, of course." Stephanie grinned at me.

"The second thing is that people will tell you to be true to yourself and expect people to accept you for who you are. That's true. But don't kid yourself into thinking *everybody* will accept you for who you are. The world is tougher than that. Sorry, but there are people out there who will hurt you and maybe even hate you for who you are.

"So I guess the only thing I can say is this: find the ones who won't. And when you do, hang on tight and never take them for granted!"

Stephanie posted the "interview" on the MyLibrary page, where Mrs. Weston loaded all the radio podcasts and student Blogs on Books. There wasn't anything really heroic about what I'd done because most people didn't listen to Potts County Middle School FM Radio.

That night I sent Tanya and Emily a text telling them to listen to the most recent program. They both said okay, and I waited on the edge of my bed, biting my nails.

Half an hour later my phone beeped.

UR a nut. I've known U went back 2
doing the FMM thing 4 a while. So
has Emily. I was waiting 4 U 2 tell me.
Course I forgive U. OK @ first I was
upset but Emily told me I was being

stupid. U were just trying 2 help pple.
& yesterday I heard Mandy talking to
Aliya about what U did 4 me. Giving up
UR invyt 2 her party. That wuz so sweet
of U. i don't know anybody who stands
up 4 others like U do.

I grinned madly as I read and reread her
text.

Emily had also sent me a text:

I know UR msg was 4 tanya but just
want U 2 know its all cool with me.
Always has been ☺☺☺

The three of us stayed up late texting each
other.

Chapter 26

I was pretty sure that not a single person in class understood what Majur had been through. Not even Ms. Pria. Until ten thirty-five on Monday morning. It was at that moment that a tiny window of insight opened into Majur's life. And if the rest of the class felt like me, they'll probably never be the same again.

After calling the roll Ms. Pria told us we were going to read parts of *The Secret Garden* before doing a comprehension exercise. Omar was handing out the class set of books. Ms. Pria had ordered us not to talk, and the class was silent except for the sound of Omar placing the books on each desk. Suddenly the quiet was interrupted by the blaring, piercing sound of the fire alarm.

Majur, who was sitting near the window, screamed, leaped out of his chair, and scrambled under his desk, covering his head with his arms. Nobody—not Chris, Ty, A. J., or Tony—said a word. We all sat, horrified, searching Ms. Pria's face for an explanation. Majur was sobbing loudly. Ms. Pria rushed toward him, yelling out to us above the sound of the siren to line up in front of the classroom door in single file. Nobody argued with her.

Then Mr. Muñoz's voice came over the loudspeaker reminding teachers that nobody was to leave their classroom, that they were testing the fire alarm. The alarm stopped. I looked over at Ms. Pria. Her face was filled with guilt and frustration.

She lifted Majur up off the floor. His hands were still over his ears. "Omar, finish handing out the books. I want silent reading for the next fifteen minutes."

She led Majur outside the classroom.

We were too stunned to talk.

~

Majur didn't come to class for the rest of
the day. I asked Ms. Pria where he was and
she said he'd gone home early but that he'd
be back tomorrow.

There were murmurs in class all day. Why
had Majur flipped out like that? What had
he gone through that he'd be scared of a
fire alarm? Would he come back to school?
Tanya suggested to Emily and me that when
he returned we could take him aside and
explain fire drills to him.

Emily scrunched up her nose. "I don't think
that's such a good idea. The teachers will probably do that now anyway. If *we* do it, Majur
might feel even worse about what happened."

Emily was right. If there was one thing I
knew about Majur it was that he didn't like
being treated differently. If we acted like we
felt sorry for him, that would make him feel
even more alone and out of place.

"Let's just see what happens when he gets
back," I said.

But Majur didn't come to class the next day.

꙳

The following day when the bell rang, we lined up in front of our classroom waiting for Ms. Pria to unlock the door and let us in. She was waiting for the second bell to signal that we could enter class. The rule was that you couldn't be in classrooms before the second bell. A couple of kids were racing to join the line before the second bell. If they arrived after it rang, Ms. Pria could give them a late slip.

As we waited I looked at the class window. It was bright and colorful, covered with our artwork and certificates with notices like 100% Attendance in Term 1, or I Participated in the Walkathon! My favorite was the certificates in the shape of bees for I Caught You *Bee*ing Good! Those were handed out when a teacher saw you doing something nice, like picking up trash without being asked, or sitting quietly with your "listening ears clicked on" during assembly. I wondered what Majur must have thought of all this. How strange and weird it must seem.

I looked around but I couldn't see him. The second bell rang and we filed into class. When the last kid, Jackson, rushed in, Ms. Pria went to close the door but Chris suddenly appeared, jamming it with his foot. He was holding a large tray of cupcakes decorated in green and white icing with little edible soccer balls on top of each one.

"I couldn't run to make it before the bell because of these," he said, motioning to the cupcakes. "It's my birthday today." Chris grinned, and Ms. Pria smiled at him.

"Okay, well, I'll make an exception for your lateness seeing as it's your birthday and you've brought everybody a treat."

Majur was right behind Chris, panting heavily. He must have been running to make it in time too. I knew Majur had heaps of late slips, even with Ms. Pria giving him lots of chances, because he was still getting used to arriving on time.

"Sorry, I late," he said, walking in behind Chris. "I . . . I was helping Chris . . . um . . . with the cake."

Chris shot Majur a look of surprise. Majur didn't flinch. He just stared back at Chris. Slowly, Chris's face broke out into a grin.

"Yeah, he was helping me," he said. "I thought I'd drop them so I asked him to walk with me in case I did. My mom stayed up late making them. She'd kill me if I wrecked them."

Majur smiled to himself. It looked to me like Ms. Pria knew what they were up to, but she took the tray of cupcakes from Chris and put them on her desk.

"Okay, Chris. And Majur, you're off the hook today too," she said. "But *only* today. Now take your seats."

"Thanks, Miss," Majur said gratefully.

"What happened to you yesterday?" Chris asked as they passed my seat. I froze, praying Chris wasn't going to say something nasty to Majur, or that Majur would get upset.

But Majur looked almost relieved that Chris had asked him. "I slept too long. Then I could not feel like coming school. *Every* day. They want us *every* day." He shook his head, bewildered. "It's *so* much."

"Tell me about it." Chris groaned.

"What's a hook?" Majur asked Chris, sitting down at the table beside mine. Chris sat at the table in front.

"Huh?" Chris said, turning to face Majur.

"Ms. Pria said we're 'off the hook.'"

I covered my mouth with my hand so they couldn't see me grinning.

"Don't know exactly," Chris said, puzzled. "I guess it just means you're not in trouble."

Majur smiled. "So if I say you're *on* the hook at soccer at lunchtime today does that make sense?"

Chris grinned. "Yeah. It makes sense. But it's not gonna happen."

Majur grinned back. "Okay. We'll play. And we'll see. I will try less hard because your birthday and you must not be on the hook too much."

Chris let out a hoot of laughter. "This is going to be fun."

And that's how Majur and Chris finally became friends.

"Do you want me to show you a cool trick you can do with a straw?" Emily asked in class. We were working in groups answering a quiz on ancient Egypt.

"Sure," I said with a smile. Emily grinned back at me and then flattened the end of the straw between her teeth and took a pair of scissors out of her pencil case. She cut the end in the shape of a V and then, when she was sure Ms. Pria's back was turned to us, she clenched the straw tightly between her lips and blew. The straw let out a horrible, *loud* sound. We clamped our hands over our ears but burst out laughing.

Ms. Pria immediately turned around. "What was that noise?"

Emily quickly hid the straw in her lap and pretended to be concentrating on her work. She sneaked a peek at Tanya and me, grinned, and winked. Tanya burst into laughter and I couldn't help but giggle too.

I realized then that it'd been a long time since I'd made Tanya laugh. Because I'd been too busy helping other people. Not just because I cared about them, but because it had made me feel good about myself. Because when I was in control of other people I could forget that I couldn't control my own friendships. That friendship wasn't something you *controlled*.

Emily hadn't stolen Tanya from me. Tanya didn't belong to me. Tanya chose to step away from me because I'd turned my back on her.

There was a reason Emily Wong's personality was like the color white.

When you mix white with any color it lightens the original color. And that's what Emily did with people, especially Tanya. She made her laugh and raised her spirits.

And there was no reason why the three of us couldn't laugh together.

After all, my personality was like the color black. Not just because, once upon a time, I thought I had power in the playground, but because if you mix black with another color, suddenly there's a shadow. I think I gave people shadows to hide in when they were hurting and lonely. When they needed privacy and space away from the glaring rainbow of the playground. But that only works for so long.

It was time for me to come out of my own shadow of fear and insecurity and remember that I loved Tanya and Emily. And that they loved me.

acknowledgments

Dyan Blacklock, Gina Inverarity, Celia Jellett: it is a joy working with you all. Thank you to my agent, Sheila Drummond, who understands me so well, and thank you to Desiree Sinclair and Sally Ahmed for their advice. Some of the inspiration for this book came to me when I was running a creative writing workshop with students at the Immigration Museum in Melbourne, Australia, as part of the Melbourne Writers Festival. I would like to thank the students and the Immigration Museum for offering me such a stimulating day.